The Sidewalk

A short novel

by

Glenn F. Higgins

Disclaimer

If you think you see yourself in this story, or think anyone you know or even knew, you must be mistaken, because this story is entirely fiction. Many of the settings are in the coastal towns of Scituate and Cohasset, Massachusetts where this writer was born and nearly educated. Venues have been scrambled and fictional characters are typical. The plot, and characters, again, are entirely made up.

Published by LULU Press
Lulu Content ID # 10626967

ISBN: 978-1-257-71572-5

Cover and back designed by James L. Voris

Acknowledgments

Of course my deepest gratitude is for my wife of the last fifty six years, who unselfishly provides encouragement and assistance on any task I have undertaken.

Secondly, I give the fine members of Pine Island Writers Inc., located here on my southwest Florida retirement island, my sincere appreciation. Without this group's assistance and helpful critiques I would have been lost.

James Voris, one of these members, provided timely guidance in navigating computer programs that I'd never been aware of, let alone known how to manage.

Accolades also to my editor, Martha Jeffers of Ft. Myers Florida.

Lastly I'd like to express thanks to a life-long friend now living on another island at the opposite corner of our great country. His steadfast friendship, encouragement, and even his contentiousness causes me to wonder how I've been so blessed.

Contents

Prologue

In the seventh grade, one bully became increasingly menacing to some of us students. He especially singled out one boy for his most terrifying looks, jabs, and punches whenever the teachers weren't looking. This torment began in the lower classes, and by the seventh grade, Dickey's taunts and abuse became so intolerable the boy became obsessed with planning ways of defending himself. He dreamed about turning the tables one day by knocking him out, smashing his face, or somehow teaching him a lesson so he would lay off. He even referred to him in vile, derogatory terms, not to his face, not to anyone else, just to himself.

By the fall of 1947, the bully's tactics grew more vicious. He would often ambush the boy if he caught him walking home from school alone. Several hundred yards of dense woods grew along one side of the road halfway between the school and the boy's house. Among the trees were large rock maples like the ones used for collecting syrup in early spring. The edge of these woods was a common place for Dickey to launch an attack on his victim as he walked home from classes. At the time, our town was in the process of rebuilding the entire sidewalk from the school, past the trees, and on to the center of town a mile away. The broken macadam footpath fronting the woods had been removed, and new wooden forms were in place to receive the concrete. Autumn was nearly over. Orange and gold leaves littered the ground, softly blanketing freshly graded fill between the forms.

Returning home from school on a wet cloudy October afternoon and fearing another chase and possible assault, the boy cut across several backyards hoping to quietly pass through the darkening woods between the road and the railroad tracks. As he made his way through the dense growth of trees, his skin suddenly prickled as he heard or possibly imagined his tormentor sneaking up from behind. Frozen to the spot for a moment, he listened, barely breathing. The silence of the damp woods was broken only by the flutter of a few colorful leaves clinging to their branches a while longer. He began to advance ever so slowly, tip-toeing through the wet brush while he withdrew a piece of metal rod kept in his book bag for protection. This twelve-inch-long-section of three- quarter-inch reinforcing bar had been in the bag for over a year. He had contemplated using it before, but never dared. Footsteps suddenly exploded behind him, electrifying his whole body. In a flash he struck his tormentor beside the head as they both crashed to the ground. The boy rolled to one side, and with the rod still clutched in his hand, readied himself for an attack. It never came. The snapping of a lone branch pierced the stillness as he stared at his prostrate attacker with horror and disbelief. Then he ran. He ran to the road. He ran all the way home. By the time he arrived, daylight was fading and the late afternoon chill enveloped him. He made an excuse about coming down with a cold to avoid his mom and dad's inquisition and headed straight to bed. They soon came in expressing concern, but the room's darkness masked his demeanor well. Satisfied, they retreated to the living room. For a long while he lay awake replaying the events in his mind. He wondered if Dickey was dead or just unconscious. He imagined his tormentor appearing in school the next day and attacking him, or would he have learned his lesson? Back and forth, back and forth, all night long, every scenario, again and again. Sleep finally smothered anxiety a few hours before dawn.

The new day arrived crisp and clear, with glistening white frost covering the ground. The boy wondered what danger would overtake him on such a glorious day. Although dreading his return to school, curiosity prevailed and he began the long walk. Half expecting Dickey to be lying in wait somewhere along the road, he favored the side across from the woods with no sidewalk. The police were at school when he arrived. Officers were asking questions about Richard Baxter's disappearance. They seemed to believe he may have run away from home again. The boy wasn't about to volunteer anything, even if asked. That's it. Just keep quiet and maybe this all will go away.

Two days later, he sneaked out of the house after midnight, returning to the woods with a flashlight and his dad's shovel and hoe. The body lay on the cold ground nearly where it had fallen. The unexpected sight of so much dried blood on Dickey's face and clothes stunned the boy. After trying unsuccessfully to dig in the heavily rooted soil, he rolled and dragged the bloated body to the edge of the newly constructed sidewalk forms. Between them he dug and scraped a hole in the fresh dirt, ducking behind a large maple when headlights approached. Fortunately, there were few vehicles late at night, and the digging in recently disturbed soil between the forms was relatively easy. As he dragged the body into the shallow grave, the boy didn't notice the 38-caliber revolver slip from Dickey's pocket and come to rest at the bottom of the hole. After scattering leaves over the tamped fill, the boy cautiously slipped past the streetlights and arrived home. He rinsed his arms and legs behind the house with the garden hose, dried himself with the dog's towel from the clothesline, and crept back to bed.

Once the police investigation began, recent animosity between Dickey and one of his former friends was discovered. Benjamin Griffin, a year older and a grade ahead of the Baxter boy, was by all accounts a close friend until the two were caught during a break-in and theft of jewelry and cash from one of the upscale homes. Their friendship appeared severely fractured, with threats of bodily harm tossed between the two of them outside the police station following one of their interrogations.

Considered first time offenders, the boys got off with probation. For a brief time, revenge by Griffin was considered a possible motive for Baxter's disappearance. Without hard evidence, this remained only conjecture. The consensus eventually settled on running away. The possibility of kidnapping was discounted when demands for a ransom never materialized. A year later the case became history, just another tragic disappearance.

In what seemed like an eternity, actually only four days after burying the body, the concrete was completed. Two years later I noticed fractures beginning and a slight depression where I remembered digging.

Following those frightening days, I went through prolonged bouts of indescribable remorse, guilt, and extreme terror at the possibility of being discovered. My slender frame became even thinner, as school grades dropped to new lows. My parent's concern was secondary, however, as their attention focused on my seventeen-year-old sister, who was becoming increasingly involved with the wrong crowd. Lucky for me, I guess, their distraction forced me to rationalize the situation myself, and I placed most of the blame on Dickey's behavior. I considered my action self-defense and reasoned little personal responsibility. The matter was closed in my own mind and remained so until adulthood. After ten or so years, thoughts of guilt began seeping into my conscience. I first pushed these aside, burying them under life's daily hustle. As I approached middle age, I found myself spending more time contemplating my secret, which eventually led to considering disclosure. After my wife's passing early in our retirement, the time had arrived. I would return to my birthplace and confess everything to the authorities.

One

The jumbo jet's roar drops to a whisper as we descend on our final approach. Skimming the rooftops of Winthrop, we target our runway at Logan International in East Boston. I plan to pick up a reserved car at the rental agency, signed out for one month. I can always renew it. As we glide toward touchdown, my thoughts drift back to that dreary day in the woods. My determination to confess involvement in Baxter's disappearance is stronger now than ever, and I will see this through. With flaps extended and thrust adjustments made, the big plane contacts the runway with a dull thud. The engines roar. A young hostess parrots a welcome message from the forward cabin, ending with the reminder to "fly with us again."

Boston traffic hasn't improved. Exiting the multi-lane overpass that converges at the Sumner Tunnel's many toll booths may be old hat for city residents, but for the occasional visitor, the scramble is unnerving. Side view mirrors lay crushed on the pavement, attesting to near misses. Another hour and a half passes before I reach my hometown.

Fifty years have evaporated since that terrible fall day. The Baxter family must have taken his sudden disappearance hard, especially having never known what really happened. I've always wondered how they resolved this in their own minds. I picture his little sister Annie, several years behind me in school.

She was a beautiful child, but seeing her looking so lost five days a week bothered me more than her brother buried under the sidewalk. I was certainly happy to move to Florida three years later. What a relief! Mom and Dad must have wondered why I was so anxious to go.

Damn red light! The town has really changed with traffic lights and all the new stores. Probably few old-timers would know me now. This place looks like a city, for God's sake. A new police station, too. Bet taxes are sky high with all the new infrastructure and social spending. There's the old Phillips place, looks smaller than I remember. Wonder who that is pruning the hedge? Wow, could that be Tommy? I've got to double back for another look. While making a turn in the middle of the road, I hear someone's horn. Aw, blow it out your ear! Can't even make a U-turn without some idiot blasting his horn. He's still there. It does look like it might be Tom. I've got to check this out. Stopping at the end of the driveway, I call out. "Hey mister, you lived here all your life?"

"So far. Who you lookin for?"

"You must be Tommy Phillips then."

"Was, the last time I looked."

"Thought it was you. Remember Holt Tilden back in junior high school?"

"And I bet you're him. Where in hell have you been all this time?"

"The whole family pulled up and moved to Florida in 1950. I've been living there ever since, raised a family and retired."

"Welcome home. What brings you back to this little town of ours?"

"Not so little anymore I'd say. Came back to settle some old business."

"Must be real old. You ain't been in town for fifty years, have ya?"

"That's about right except for passing through once or

twice. Tell me, what are the barricades for? They're clustered along Country Way beyond where the old grade school used to be."

"The town finally got around to approving money to rebuild that old concrete sidewalk. It's been broken up for years, mostly from them big tree roots, I reckon."

I've got to cut this short. I need to check into the motel and get something to eat before I drop in my tracks.

"I gotta keep moving, Tommy. Nice to see you. Maybe we'll catch up later."

"Hope we will anytime, anytime. You know where to find me. Gimme some notice, I'll get a couple of guys together if you want."

"Sounds good to me. Whenever its convenient with you is OK. I'm staying at the Colonial."

Tom is a dead ringer for his old man, tall, gray, and string beanie.

Back in the car, I proceed on Country Way toward Dickey's grave as if drawn by some magnetic force. It should be around this bend. The terrain looks different. Most of the huge trees are gone. The concrete is terribly broken and heaved due to old roots. I wonder why this section wasn't replaced sooner.

The winding road passes fields of wildflowers and corn, eventually bringing me to the harbor front where I spent most summers fishing and sailing. The draggers are all offshore, leaving the commercial pier temporarily available to locals and visitors. Two boys about thirteen are threatening to toss another kid's bicycle over the edge. Adults pretend to ignore the ruckus. One gentleman in a business suit attempts to lower a sailboat mast to a boat tied below the edge of the pier using the fishermen's derrick. My curiosity in witnessing the outcome is overpowered by hunger, so I leave, searching for a place for lunch.

A small eatery named "Copper Bucket," sandwiched between two eighteenth century brick edifices, welcome me with a harbor-view table complete with condiments and a fresh roll of paper towels on a stick. My wife's nutritional training controlling me, I settle for the Caesar salad with shrimp and unsweetened ice tea, no dessert. There are seven patrons scattered among the ten little tables, all but two of them wolfing down the last vestiges of an orange-colored entrée I guess to be the "Lasagna Special." The other two diners, male and female, sit across from each other at the table inside the three-over-five windowed front door. Both appear to be close to my age, and I wonder if they are original townies. I can't avoid studying people, looking for something familiar in their faces tying them to the past. I recognize nothing in these two. Slowly eating my salad, I gaze out the rear window overlooking the lazy harbor scene. A small boy, that I judge to be about twelve, sails below my window in his little "Rookie" sailboat. For a moment I'm a twelve year old sailing in the same harbor, waiting for the other kids in their boats to join me racing to the beach behind the channel. Visual images beyond the glass become overlaid by my imagined sequence of events awaiting me in this town. Will I be immediately arrested after my confession? Might there be a trial? I'm sure I would be granted bail, but how will the townsfolk react? I believe the majority of residents are either new or too young to know anything about the boy's disappearance so many years before. I'm mainly concerned about the judgment of my peers, and of what may lie ahead. Leaving the restaurant, I remain confident my decision will prevail.

As I slide into my car, something yellow tucked under the windshield wiper catches my eye. Opening the door again, I reach for the paper. Irritated, I find a parking violation notice with the word "hydrant" underlined. I see the yellow pipe plainly now in my rear-view mirror. Someone must have removed the trash barrels blocking its location after I parked here an hour ago. I open the glove compartment and fold the notice over the lip before closing it. This will be a reminder. I have bigger things to attend to first.

It's time to return to the Colonial where my bags sit unpacked. On entering the room, I find the message light blinking. Inquiring by phone, I am directed to the manager's desk where I retrieve a handwritten note left an hour before. It's an invitation to attend a cookout the following afternoon with some old friends at Tom Phillip's place. As this is Friday and I plan to do my business the following week, I am pleased at the prospect and phone my acceptance.

Saturday morning I fine-tune my letters to the kids. These are the letters I have been putting off for years. I confided only to my wife the details of Dickey's demise, and that was eight years after we married. I had begun their letter on my computer almost a year ago but was never able to finish it. Time is running out, and I am determined to have them in the mail by Monday. How many times had I attempted to share this terrible secret with them, only to seek shelter in benign banter? I know receiving these will be unsettling for them both, but it must be done.

September 4, 2002
Dear Michael and Sally,
Time has passed slowly for me since your mother passed away twenty eight months ago. I know you miss her, as I do. It's almost more than I can bear. My greatest comfort now is seeing both of you happily rooted in your families and daily activities. You need not be concerned about my future, as I have enough monetary reserves to survive quite well. There is, however, something I must now confess to you both—something which has pained me for many years. Your mother is the only person I have ever shared my agony with. Long ago, we both decided to shield both of you during your childhood years, putting off disclosure until later.

When I was thirteen years old, I accidentally killed another boy. He was a threatening bully who fell when I struck him with a metal rod in self-defense. One strike was all I provided, but unfortunately, it was a mortal blow. I later buried his body. He was reported missing, and no one, not even my parents, ever knew or suspected what happened. Our family moved to Florida three years later, and the boy's disappearance was never resolved.

Today I am back at my birthplace, where the incident happened. I have wrestled with this nearly all my life, more so as I get older. I don't want to live another year with this suffocating burden weighing me down. I am going to inform the authorities and admit my complicity in the boy's disappearance. I will attend to this in the coming weeks. I hope you will forgive me for causing you stress and concern at this time, but I am determined to see it through. Please keep this in strict confidence until I have spoken to the authorities. I have not retained counsel and am unaware what my legal standing will be. I am presently staying at the Colonial Motel. The address is on the envelope. I have arranged for the proprietor to process my mail for the rest of this month, and you have my cell phone number.

Don't worry about me. I love you both and will fill you in as things develop.

Please say hello from Grandpa to the kids.

Love,

Dad

With no excuse to delay this any longer, I drop both letters into the mailbox outside the motel. In the lobby I feed quarters into the vending machines until a ham and cheese sandwich and a root beer tumble out. I take my lunch to be consumed in the car as I search vaguely familiar terrain for childhood memories.

Traveling northwest, I approach the "highway." Seventy-five years earlier this two-lane road was built by the State of Massachusetts to reroute Cape Cod traffic west of the Boston Post Road, connecting the small villages along the seashore. In the fifties, we referred to this as "the new road." Mature maple and beech trees now reach over the pavement to the center, likening the road to a rabbit trail.

Alden Evan once lived on the corner of Bay Hill Road and the new road. He lived with his mom, dad, and sister in the tiny box-like bungalow perched precariously high on a glacially formed ledge overlooking both roads. When I was a teenager, this house seemed more fragile than surrounding New England homes. As I approach the intersection, the house and yard appear smaller than I remember. Enormous trees all but obscure the building. Two 70's era, apparently unregistered, rusty sedans lounge beneath the ledge. Two shirtless young men are apparently resuscitating a similarly aged pickup, the front end held aloft with a chain-fall hung from one of the oak tree's limbs. Although the Evan house was small, it had been kept orderly. Seeing it disheveled this way saddens me.

A half mile down the highway from Alden's house was our favorite camping ground, locally referred to as the Pit. A crooked dirt road extended from the highway, a quarter mile in to an abandoned gravel pit, unused since the road construction fifteen years earlier. The leftover terrain looked like something out of the old west, with expanses of flat gravel interrupted by brush-covered hills. A scattering of small trees grew in the hollows prone to collect rain. We used a vine to swing ourselves into the water from a white oak tree. This small pond, the result of a hole left by the road builders, became our private swimming pool. Ten feet at its deepest, the east end tapered to a shallow cattail swamp. Water snakes were common and we avoided them. The largest frogs were caught by cannon-balling from the elevated bank beside the grassy road, and we cooked the legs like the soldiers did in my older brother's book, "How to Survive on Land and Sea." The dirt road is still here. I cautiously drive the car through lumpy potholes, splashing mud to each side as the undercarriage scuffs the grassy middle. The rim of the Pit appears densely covered with fifty-year and older trees. Gone is the open expanse of gravel. The pond has evolved into a stagnant swamp with dense vegetation blanketing most of the surface. The giant oak tree has toppled its rotting limbs, halfway submerged in the muck.

Scratching through some scrub near the rotting roots of the old oak, I look for another connection to my past. With a broken pine branch in one hand, I slash and poke in the weeds until I strike something solid. It's a rock, but not the one I am looking for. I prod some more until finally discovering the stone I'm after. I sweep the dead brush and twigs aside, pulling the remaining grass away with my fingers. A flat piece of shale, a foot wide, protrudes from the soil at a forty-five-degree angle. Only part of the crudely scratched letters show above ground. Digging into the soil, displacing fifty years of composted vegetation with my hands, I uncover the rest of the inscription: PUP-1945. Tears flood my eyes as I kneel beside the grave.

Pup was our dog. Actually, I thought of him as my dog because I never had one of my own. He appeared out of the bushes soon after Alden and I discovered this swimming hole early in the summer of '41. He was a friendly young black mongrel with no collar or identification, so we decided to adopt him. Whenever we arrived at the Pit, he would appear out of the bushes and stay with us until we left for dinner. As we walked our bikes down the dirt road to the highway, Pup would follow, but then vanish into the bush as we neared the traffic. I once brought him home using a piece of clothesline and collar, only to have him disappear when unrestrained and then greet us when we returned to the Pit. I thought the dog must have a home in one of the properties to the west, someplace close enough to hear or smell us when we arrived. He seemed to want friends, and we were happy to have him. The three of us enjoyed that first summer, swimming, camping, and exploring the dense woods to the north. When winter came, I rode my bicycle to the Pit several times, calling his name and getting no response. Disappointed, I considered him lost forever.

The following June, Pup greeted us on our very first visit. He had grown larger over the winter, assuring us he must have a caring home. Alden wanted to change his name to something more suitable for a big dog, but I prevailed, and he remained "Pup." Many delightful hours were spent whiling away the summer. By early September our visits became infrequent due to school obligations and the cooling temperatures. By then Pup would accompany us all the way to the edge of the highway as we departed. He would sit on the shoulder and watch us fade into the distance. We assumed he would then scurry off through the bushes for home.

On our last fall visit, we lost track of time and I realized I would be late for dinner. In our rush to leave, I forgot to pick up my new jacket that lay on the ground beside the big oak. By the time I discovered it was missing, I was already home. My mother was upset by my carelessness, but I told her I knew where it was and considering it was already dark, assured her it would be safe until the next day.

The following morning was Saturday, so after breakfast I jumped on my bike and arrived at the Pit road twenty minutes later. I was surprised to see Pup lying on my jacket as I approached the big oak. My delight turned to concern when he didn't jump up and come running toward me. He was acting strangely, with his head on my jacket and ears laid back. When I reached him I found dried blood over most of the jacket and fresh blood seeping from his midsection. When he looked into my face, I knew he was dying. I laid my hands on his body and his eyes closed—within minutes he was gone. I held him and cried for an hour. When I walked my bike to the highway, I could see traces of blood all the way to the edge of the road. I guessed that he must have been hit by a car while watching us leave the previous afternoon.

Alden and I buried Pup in this place near the oak tree. We attempted to find the actual owner by placing a notice in the local paper. When no one came forward, I carved his name on a piece of flagstone to mark his grave. As I leave, I remember the good times we had so long ago, and I'm happy to have been reunited with the memory of my dog.

It is mid-afternoon by the time I return to the Colonial. I decide to take a nap before getting ready for the cookout. As I lie on the bed, I wonder who the people are that Tommy has corralled for the evening. He hadn't given clues when I inquired during my acceptance call. This was going to be interesting. I try to recall various faces from my childhood and soon fall asleep.

On awakening, the bedside clock glows ten minutes after four. I am expected at Tom's by 5:00, so have no time to waste. Showered, shaved, and deodorized, I arrive at 5:15, close enough I think.

Tom greets me on the porch, and we quickly pass through the house to the backyard where other guests are gathered. At first glance I recognize no one. There are seven people besides myself, Tom, with his wife Arlene, whom I have never met. George Cliff, short, balding, hefty, and bespectacled, doesn't resemble the Georgie I knew. This changes, however, as he speaks with a Long Island accent absorbed from his parents and earliest surroundings. As we talk, his unfamiliar features melt, revealing the boy I had known. Ted Anderson introduces himself. Lean and tall, he was and still is a runner, he claims. Our association in junior high was mainly through the track team to which we both belonged. After our introduction I can clearly see he is a matured Ted I had known before. Next in line is a married couple, both artists who began their relationship in junior high school. Bob Hendricks and his wife, Adele, recently celebrated their forty- second anniversary. I barely remember Adele, but Bob was one of my closest harbor-rat friends during school vacations. I would prefer to spend more time with Bob, but defer this when another gentleman in the corner draws my attention. The elderly man has been talking with the woman assisting Arlene with food preparations. He sits uncomfortably in his wheelchair as I move across the patio to greet him. A full head of gray and black shaggy hair is crunched against his blue

Polo shirt collar. As I approach, I notice oxygen tubes in place below sunken eyes that reveal no joy in life. Introducing himself as Alden Evan, I cannot at first reconcile his scrawny frame and deeply lined facial features. He informs me he has terminal cancer among a myriad of other health issues. To my surprise he is still living in the old homestead on the ledge overlooking the highway, sharing the place with his only, and still unmarried son. It must have been this son and his friends who were working on the pickup hours before.

"I'm glad to see anyone nowadays," Alden whispered. "Doc says I got another month or two, the sooner the better I'd say."

I am tempted to bring up the good times at the Pit, but hold back to avoid reminding him of Pup's demise. I hang with Alden for some time, attempting to console him, but he will have none of it. Tom rescues me after an appropriate spell and small talk ensues among the others, with me taking a ribbing for wearing shoes covered with mud like I had been clamming. I begin to wonder how something like that sticks in their memories, when I had long ago forgotten.

"Chow's on!" yells Tom.

One by one, the guests serve themselves and find seats. Arlene's helper emerges from the kitchen and joins the group. Ann Carlson, Arlene's closest friend, lost her husband two years before. Both of them have resided in town their entire lives. Ann looks several years younger than the other guests, but she seems to know them all. Tom says she had volunteered to help Arlene with the preparations the previous day. There's something about Ann that sparks my interest. She is sixtyish and trim, and an exceptionally beautiful woman with impeccable personal neatness. I cannot fathom why, but the attraction seems magnetic. While attempting to mask my affected self from the others, I can't keep my eyes off her.

This pleasant day soon ebbs as the sun slips below the tree line. Mosquitoes quickly invade the patio, forcing guests toward their cars with goodbye waves and promises to reconvene. Ann Carlson stays on to assist with the cleanup. Tom suggests we move to the living room. Once he settles into the large stuffed leather chair, I study his features, recognizing characteristics leftover from childhood. He is still as skinny as a post, but what had been a smooth, light complexion has grown ruddy and deeply furrowed. I am reminded of honest Abe, thick dark hair and all. I purposely engage him in small talk until the women finish and join us in the living room. Conversation then turns to anecdotes about school days long passed.

"I remember you practicing on the cross country track team," Tom began.

"That was junior high. We would run through the churchyard, then the cemetery, and around the track," I reply.

"You know, the environmentalists recently forced the school to change their practice course and claimed the kids were running too close to a possible habitat of endangered species," Tom said. "The woods are full of deer, turkey, and coyotes. No one alive today remembers any of them being here before, and there weren't nearly as many people living here."

"If there's anything endangered, I'd think they'd be trampled or eaten by the proliferation of new critters," I surmise. "Is the no-hunting rule still in effect east of the highway?"

Tom answers in the affirmative. "We've got coyotes running away with small dogs, some of them with their leashes still attached. We got deer destroying people's vegetable gardens and jumping in front of cars, but we can't shoot a firearm this side of 3A—the anti-hunting crowd has this state all tied up. I have to go to New Hampshire for venison."

Idle talk eventually turns to families. After Tom's commentary, carefully edited by Arlene, Ann begins.

"I grew up on Vine Street near the old grade school. I was a Baxter before Eddy Carlson came to town and swept me off my feet."

I sit glued to my chair, conscious of pressure pulsing in my neck and throat and my heart pounding furiously. The room seems devoid of anything but the sound of her voice as visions of her brother's lifeless body flash before me. Ann continues as my attention wanders. In my mind, pieces of the past come and go. No one seems to sense my altered state, and I somehow feel safe from inquiries. I rejoin the conversation, but wonder how strange it is that I came to this place and of my attraction to this woman. Determined as I am to further some sort of relationship, I realize the time is getting late. I express appreciation for the evening and leave for the motel with no idea how I will proceed with Ann Baxter Carlson.

Two

On awakening, I find mottled blue and white patterned wallpaper two feet from my face. I study the colors before realizing where I am. Heavy truck engines whine as operators downshift the diesel rigs descending the long grade in front of the motel. My watch agrees with the bedside clock: 8:30 am. I gradually focus on the previous evening's gathering, where I sat muted during Ann Carlton's shocking revelation. Rationalizing my interest was elusive. Something urges me to devise some way to kindle a relationship with this woman. A shave and shower bring no easy answers, so I leave for breakfast at the harbor with no clue as to my next move.

The restaurant where I had lunch the previous afternoon beckons me for another meal. At 9:15 in the morning, the place is a madhouse. Tables are filled with early Sunday walkers and late arriving fishermen. Luckily, the same table against the window becomes vacant. A pretty waitress, looking to be in her thirties and dressed in pink, approaches.

"Good morning to you. Would you like coffee?"

"Good morning, young lady. I would like two fried eggs over medium, bacon, dark toast, and coffee with cream, please."

"Orange juice?"

"Not today, thank you."

While waiting for the meal I begin to think my approach to Ann would best be done through Arlene Phillips. Try as I might, I cannot think of another plan that is reasonable. I believe a "thank-you call" to Tom and Arlene this afternoon is not only in order, but may present some kind of opening that I cannot now imagine.

When breakfast arrives, I jump at the sudden thud of my coffee mug hitting the table. Its contents spill across the place-mat and into my lap. My waitress stands with her mouth wide open. I notice she has perfect teeth.

"Oh, I am *so* sorry. Let me clean this up. Here, use these napkins from the other table while I get you another cup. I didn't scald you, did I? I'm *really* sorry."

"No harm done, miss. If I could exchange this chair, though, for one without a coffee puddle, I'd appreciate it."

We make the swap and I sit down in my soggy pants, the temperature already cooled enough so they just feel warm. I push off my right shoe, and wave my foot under the table to dry.

Breakfast arrives, along with more apologies from the still-blushing waitress, who tells me there won't be any charge for my meal. I try to reassure her no lasting harm resulted from the spill except to the crease in my trousers, which I believe will return following the next wash cycle. I notice the crowd has thinned by the time I place a generous tip beside the check marked "no charge" in neat letters across the middle. As I stand, the sudden chill of wet pants reminds me to request some plastic bags before leaving the restaurant. I intend to prevent my "take-out" coffee from saturating the car seat.

After showering and changing, I leave my lodging and drive along the beach road enjoying the crisp blue sky extending all the way to the horizon. In shallow pools along the beach, fan-like patterns of wavelets rush here and there, driven by gusty blasts of northwest wind. I arrive at the old lighthouse at the northern breakwater protecting the harbor and village. Once an important aid to navigation, the lighthouse outlived its intended use long ago. Reduced candlepower now shortens its visual range to a harbor beacon, and the keeper's building has become a tourist attraction run by the local historical society. There are no other vehicles in the parking lot this morning. I pull up to the beach-stone perimeter and switch off the ignition. This is a good place to contemplate my next move.

I know I must advise my children about the impending delay of my confession to the police. The kids will not have received the letters yet, so I decide to put off calling them until Tuesday. Next on my agenda is planning a sensible approach to Ann Carlson, a task not as easy as I first considered. My thoughts drift in all directions. I can't concentrate, so I think I'll call her straightaway without going through Tom and Arlene. No, this may be too direct, better to enlist them and make the approach more casual. I don't want to frighten her off. In the back of my mind, I want to gently explore the impact her brother's disappearance caused before I report my involvement to the police.

A dark-red lobster boat slowly chugs by the end of the lighthouse jetty as it heads out for a Sunday cruise. Two young boys sit on the aft deck inspecting details of their fishing poles. Their mother rummages through brightly colored plastic bags, in search of something probably left home during their hurried departure. Dad kicks the throttle forward as the boat clears the jetty and heads offshore for the day. I close my eyes as the familiar diesel's whine, and salt air surrounds me. Walking over the surf-rounded beach stones, I wonder what life would have been like, had I never moved to Florida so many years ago. Would I have resisted relocating if it weren't for Dickey's demise?

After leaving lighthouse point, I drive to the village grocery store on Front Street for several items. My scribbled notes list toothpaste, coffee lightener, and dark chocolate. As I approach the candy aisle, I come face to face with Ann Carlson.

Dressed in a stylish gold sweater, and coral colored pedal pushers, she appears even younger than she did last evening. After a shaky beginning, the conversation eases when I express my appreciation for Tom and Arlene's hospitality, even suggesting a reciprocal dinner and evening out, and would she like to join us. I am as surprised at my words as she is speechless. I assure her this is a spur-of-the-moment thing, which it surely is, and her presence would make for me a memorable evening. With enough reserve, she agrees, while I jot down her number. I promise to be in contact after setting a date and time with Tom and Arlene. Following a few more minutes of pleasantries we part, and I proceed down the aisle with no particular item in mind. A faint whiff of Prince Matchavelli's "Wind Song" floats by. I inhale deeply as she disappears around the end of the aisle. Way to go! I couldn't have planned a better approach with a stack of how-to books in each hand.

As I leave the market, thoughts of my dear deceased wife buoy my spirits. Her losing battle with cancer after forty wonderful years was devastating. I wonder if she would agree with my plan to reveal our secret. We never considered or even discussed the possibility of this confession I am about to make. I sense her agreement wash over me as I approach the car and somehow feel empowered by her memory.

I call Arlene and thank her for the delightful evening. She and Tom accept my invitation to dinner this coming Friday at The Mill House. Her hesitation when I inform her Ann will be joining us for dinner is obvious. I tell her my plans to be away early in the week and leave my cell number in case of something unexpected. I'll bet she is on the phone right now with Ann, finding out all the details. I decide to coordinate the date and time with Ann in another hour.

The social complexity created since arriving in town only three days ago concerns me. I had resolved to make my confession as straightforward as possible. Rekindling associations with old friends and the unexpected acquaintance with Dickey's sister could burden my intentions, possibly even derailing the whole plan. I have decided to drive to the Maine coast for a few days and revisit my other childhood playground. The time away will give me a chance to evaluate my options before Friday's dinner engagement.

Three

It's hard to believe this narrow two-lane road passed for a super highway back in the fifties. Traveling the Main Turnpike for the first time since college brings to mind working vacations on the coast of Maine during seasonal breaks from school. Cliff Island, a half mile off shore in Blue Hill Bay, was Uncle Lloyd's home all his life. I worked part time as stern man, helping with the trawls and repairing pots for room and board plus small change. Lloyd was a diminutive, weather-beaten, tough-as-leather codger who the locals said limped with a slight walk. When he was only fourteen, he became injured under a falling stack of lobster pots when a rogue wave rolled his dad's boat nearly fifty degrees. Joyous summers were spent with the old man, living on the island only two square miles in area. Leaving the turnpike near Falmouth Foreside, I pick up Route 1 and proceed northeast to East Orland, then south on SR176 to 175.

My late afternoon arrival brings me here in time to witness the sun streaming through the top branches of the hemlocks growing beyond the golden marsh grass. The September chill brings out sweaters and light, hooded jackets for the locals surrounding the Lobster Roll eatery next to the town's launching ramp. Four boys about eight or so play keep away with the bareheaded one's international orange cap. Two middle-aged yachtsmen, grounding their hard bottom dinghy at the water's edge, step ashore with a five-gallon pail, likely to carry freshly boiled lobsters to their yawl anchored a hundred yards out.

I get a place in the short line in front of the counter. Aware Downeasters may be shy starters, I smile at the fisherman-looking gentleman behind me and begin the conversation.

"How's the lobstering been this season?"

"Plenty lobsters, but the damn price gone to hell."

"How come so many lobsters?" I ask.

"All the natural predators around these parts been fished out or killed. Seals the only thing left."

"Looks like the market price has held up pretty much," I volunteer.

"Wouldn't be standing here if my wife wasn't behind that counter."

"What will you have mister?" from the matronly woman inside.

"Lobster roll, half fries, half onion rings and iced tea, unsweetened," I order.

"That's twenty eight dollars—pick it up and pay at the other window," she says.

I notice the lady wink at her husband standing behind me and assume I have been overcharged, being the tourist I am. Retrieving my meal from the young woman at the second window, I carry the paper tray to the fallen telephone pole lying in the grass on the south side of the boat ramp. The pole is already populated with six other diners. As I approach, I notice six cormorants perched on a dead pine branch beyond, seeming to imitate the folks sitting on the log.

With dinner consumed, I walk up the grassy hill to the River House, advertised now as a Bed and Breakfast Inn. Two noisy ten-year-old boys, one with filthy hands and grubby knees, play on the stairs leading from the worn, oriental-carpeted reception parlor to the second floor. Fifty years ago this was the only tourist lodging in town—"Al's Guest House." That six-dollar-a-night fee has climbed to ninety-five dollars plus tax, and this is the least expensive lodging in town. Nostalgia brought me here, and I decide to register for one night despite the inn's degradation. I reflect on my working years in developing countries, spending nights in remote foreign hovels that were considerably worse. With my room paid for, I walk back to the front door intending to retrieve the car I'd left down by the ramp. As I reach for the door, a sudden commotion increasing in volume causes me to grip the knob and crouch, raising my other arm in defense. The grubby-kneed kid, having tumbled down a half flight of stairs, crashes against the back of my legs. Had the door been open, we both would be sprawled on the porch.

"Sorry, mister. Are you OK?" from the thirtyish-looking woman now standing at the head of the stairs in her black bra and half slip.

"I'm all right," I reply

"Get up here now, Jack," she commands. "And apologize to the man you nearly knocked over. Look at yourself—you get up here and get into the tub right now."

"I'm sorry, mister, I gotta go and get cleaned up."

I acknowledge his apology, bid the black bra good evening, and limp down the hill to my car.

I eat twenty dollars worth of breakfast the following morning, bringing the real cost of lodging down to seventy-five dollars. Not a bad meal either, considering the turmoil in the dining room at eight o'clock. After swallowing my money's worth, I drive to the landing to secure passage on one of the private water crafts. Cliff Island's population is too insignificant to accommodate a commercial ferry, so visitors without a boat must purchase their ride from one of the locals. Payment for the half-mile run is often refused, unless the trip is dedicated for the passenger.

George Bailey, the young lobsterman carrying empty lobster boxes back to the island, is preparing to leave the float. He agrees to give me passage as soon as the boat is loaded. George is outfitted for fishing from his hundred-horse, outboard powered, flat-bottom skiff, looking like it needs to be reacquainted with the wet end of a paintbrush. Five boxes aboard, each with the capacity of a hundred pounds, seem like a bountiful day's haul from a skiff with no hydraulic slave. There's a small Briggs & Stratton gas engine driving an open-ended winch in line with the galvanized pipe davit. The starboard rail holds a series of oak slats on brackets, indicating the use of short trawls in his sets. George's broad shoulders looming over his short stocky frame suggest this isn't just a part-time job. I toss my duffel bag and tent frame into the bow and untie the painter.

"How many pots can you handle on the rail?" I ask, as we motor between the moored boats.

"Five," he answered. "When I earn enough for a real boat, I'll be able to handle ten.
Been fishing out of this skiff since I was seventeen. That was eight years ago."

His ruddy face and weathered hands confirm he takes his work seriously. Fifty years from now, if he survives that long, his leather-like skin will exhibit varying afflictions including skin cancers. I show him surgical scars on my arms and face, an attempt to suggest the need for sun protection I'm sure he will never use.

As we approach the cove marker off Cliff Island, the place looks as I remember it, except more compact. According to George, nobody winters over anymore, but the summer residential population of thirty-five hasn't changed in a hundred years. We pull alongside the float secured under the ramp extending from the rocky shoreline. He absolutely refuses my ten dollars and motors off to his berth at the far edge of the cove.

There are four small skiffs tied to the float. I can see only three people on shore before climbing the ramp to the dirt road. Seated in a weather worn captain's chair lashed to one of the galvanized eyebolts securing the ramp sits the island's general inspector. Inquiries come forth before I reach the top.

"Where you hail from mista?"

"Florida, by way of Scituate, Massachusetts."

My reply is trimmed short, by an impromptu recitation of the island's history. Clyde Bagley, looking to be in his seventies and sporting a full head of snow-white hair, pours forth snippets of the island's particulars, appropriately beginning with its discovery in the mid sixteen-hundreds. I listen to his monologue, scrutinizing it for variances to my own recollections. When I'm able to squeeze myself behind one of his long breaths, Uncle Lloyd's name is injected. This shuts him down while he cogitates for a moment. Reclaiming ground, his eyes narrow over his bushy yellow stained mustache as he points his right index finger into the air.

"Sure, I remember Lloyd Tilden. He got crushed under some pots as a youngsta, crippled him up real bad, it did. I was 'bout ten years younger than him, I'd say. He's been gone maybe twenty-five years, ain't he?"

I nod in agreement as he recalls Lloyd's kinship with some of the other island inhabitants both living and dead.

"Your uncle's house has changed hands several times, most recently to a retired couple using it as a vacation place. They boarded it up for the winta couple of weeks ago, then stuck a for-sale sign on the front lawn," he volunteered.

I inform Bagley of my earlier intentions to tent somewhere along the beach for the next two nights, and inquire if, in his opinion, anyone would mind my camping beside my uncle's cottage. He gives me assurance this will be acceptable, and he'll inform others of my connection to Lloyd and the island.

I must have telegraphed signs of leaving, for he offers his

services any time needed. This seems an appropriate opening, and thanking him, I excuse myself as I begin walking down the dusty gravel road toward Lloyd's house. I squint from the sun reflecting off the windless water below me. Inhaling the salt air, I observe the gently surging rockweed briefly exposed at low tide. Black backed seagulls fight over scraps of bait spilled on the lobster car anchored near shore. Their shrill calls echo off rocky cliffs above the small cluster of chalk-white cottages clinging to the few patches of flat ground.

The road soon elbows around an outcropping of rock where I find Uncle Lloyd's cottage, almost hidden among full-grown hemlocks. I confirm the location, as this is the nearest building to the bend. The old cottage has been extended with the addition of a screened summer porch across the entire front. Further examination indicates the rest of the structure is as originally built. In the brush behind the house I discover the rusty steel frame of his four-wheeled trailer used for moving boats on the island. The old man built the carrier from a retired International truck frame, adding padded rails, movable poppets, and tow bar. Years of rust have stolen most of the rig, leaving only remnants of the frame and wheels.

Back on the front porch, I settle on the top step and study the expansive view before me. Blue Hill Bay widens to the southeast towards Swans Island, then on to the Atlantic just over the horizon. Lloyds's lobster pots were strung across most of the bay at one time or another throughout the season. I envision my uncle hoeing the vegetable garden beside the driveway.

At twenty-two he married Emma and cared for his own dad until the gentleman passed away in the fifties. Emma died during childbirth producing a stillborn boy only three years after she and Lloyd married. He welcomed me even when I was a small boy arriving for a week's vacation with my mom and dad. During college summer vacations, I always looked forward to returning to the island.

Remnants of the new owner's vegetable garden lay

beside the driveway in the same location. The growing season is over. Three crooked beanpoles remain standing in the garden, the others already fallen across tall weeds rooted in neglected rows. Lloyd stored his poles inside the shed and added ragweed and kelp to the garden soil before turning the whole bed over for the winter. He didn't believe in chemical fertilizers.

Using my feet to kick aside fallen debris, I clear a flat area in the grass beside the cottage. I set up my small tent and roll out the sleeping bag. Food and other gear are left in the waterproof duffel bag I conveniently hang from a broken pine tree limb ten feet away. After devouring a can of salmon, a quarter of my wheat crackers, and some Gatorade, I decide to exercise and rediscover the island's allure. As I leave the cottage, I copy the "For Sale" information on a scrap of paper and place it into in my wallet.

Following the gravel road another hundred yards brings me to the end of the cottage settlement and a small plateau. A narrow stony path zigzags down the slope through wild blueberry bushes clinging to crevices in the island rock. High tides have arranged contoured rows of seaweed and flotsam near the head of the beach. I walk toward the water's edge, where shale-like chips of rock are gradually smaller, until the beach becomes coarse, gray sand. Small waves roll endlessly onto the shore from what appears to be a table-flat ocean. Extending my hand to receive the next surge, I judge the temperature at around fifty-five degrees, suitable for swimming only to save one's life. Walking the beach, observing the timeless rocks of this magnificent island, I resign myself to the fact that these few days are really for my own enjoyment. I'll need to address dinner and the commitment I have made soon enough.

The sun is descending behind the mainland trees when I return to the tent and prepare for my first night's camping in many years. The last time I'd been camping must have been with the Boy Scout troop when my son Michael was in scouting. As the sky darkens, a waxing crescent moon reflects light off the white cottage wall, dimly illuminating my campsite. Before midnight, I lay with my head outside the tent flaps in the night air, visually walking among the stars in Orion. I find the Hunting Dogs, then Procyon and Sirius before falling off.

*

I'm on a boat, on the forward deck lying on my back. Spray rakes across my face. The wind rattles the jib overhead. I raise my right arm to protect my face. My hand is slapped hard by the tattered sail.

*

The canvas I feel is my tent flap. I jolt awake in a raging storm that sneaked over the island early this morning. Hastily, I slide myself back into the confines of the lively tent and hold the two flaps together with both hands. Wind howls and rain pelts the canvas. I'm hanging on to the closed flaps wondering how I'll tie them together. With my right leg I sweep the tent floor, searching for one of my hiking boots. Dragging one from the corner with my foot, I undo the lacing with one hand while holding the flaps closed with the other. Now I hold both flaps to the ground with my knees and weave the bootlace through several grommets, and tie them around the tent pole. I find my flashlight and add the other bootlace, completing the job. The tent is a mess. I crawl back into my wet bag and try to sleep, remembering Ernest Shackleton's ordeal on the Antarctic ice. I wake up late, as sunlight leaks through the wrinkles in the jury-rigged flaps. Wisps of gray cloud scoot across the island under cirrostratus scribbles in a cobalt sky. The squall is gone. Today will be fine.

By ten thirty the wind swings southwest. My bedding hangs from clotheslines strung behind the house. The duffel bag has blown off the branch, but rain hasn't seeped in. After eating a scant breakfast, I walk back to the landing to see if the inspector is at his post. I cordially greet Mister Bagley and inquire if there is a 110-outlet I may use to charge my cell phone. He just happens to be sitting next to one at the top of the ramp.

"Sure, go ahead and charge her up."

I thank him and plug in as his inquiry begins.

"Where in hell did you sleep last night?" he asked. "Not in no tent I wager."

I affirm I was indeed in my tent, snug as a bug in a storm. I secretly don't relish being the latest main-lander heading the island's gossip column, even if they don't have a gossip column. Clyde delivers more of the island goings on and history while I wait for the phone to charge. His oratory bridges the forty years since I frequented the island. I believe after thirty minutes the phone is charged enough to call my kids, so I unplug and drop the device into my pocket. I'll call them later.

After walking down the ramp, I initiate conversation with the blond boy in coveralls who is smelting off the end of the float. About twelve years old, he fishes with two cane poles, one laying on each side of him, with two feet of the tips extending over the edge.

"Get anything?" I ask.

"About a dozen. I've been here over an hour."

He lifts the little plywood square off the plastic five-gallon pail he's been sitting on, to show off his flopping catch. The tip of his right pole dips slightly. He cautiously waits until it suddenly bends downward and rattles sideways along the float. Lifting it, he drops the pole further back on the float, landing the wire spreader with two shiny smelts onto the deck. Dropping the fish into his bucket, he hurriedly baits both hooks with tiny pieces of sea worm and the spreader is again lowered into the water while the second pole bounces furiously beside him.

"Things are pickin' up," he says.

Smelting can be a solitary endeavor. Appreciating his concentration, I express a "see you later," and amble back up the ramp. Clyde is about to leave, when I inquire about possibly renting a skiff for a bit of fishing outside the cove.

"You can use my nephew's dory for nothing. It's tied right there on the float," he says, "Jackie's off-island for a couple of days. Problem is, it's only got one oar. Can you scull?"

"Do seagulls eat fish?" I ask.

I sense his confusion so follow up with, "Yes. I can scull and appreciate your offer. I'll get my stuff and be out a couple of hours if that's OK."

Clyde assures me I may use the boat all afternoon, so I descend the ramp again and approach the young boy to buy some bait. He agrees to give up ten sea worms and two undersized smelt for three bucks. I pay the boy and tell him I'll be back in minutes to pick them up. Probing through my gear at the tent, I settle on two plastic shopping bags. I'll use one to hold bait and one for fresh fish. I grab another shirt and the new marline hand-line and tin of hooks bought from the hardware store. Johnson, the young smelt fisherman, drops the agreed bait into my bag, I untie the dory's painter and shove off.

This is not one of the Banks dorys so common in Maine. Those were originally stackable work boats deployed from fishing schooners plying the Grand Banks a century ago. My borrowed craft is a Swampscott five-strake dory with rounded bilge and graceful sheer, too nice to use as a work boat. The long oar allows easy maneuverability from either standing or sitting positions. I begin sculling out of the cove, skirting the shoreline and head toward the sandy bottom I hope is still off the eastern point. This is the flounder ground I had fished as a youngster, and I'm anxious to see if the spot still holds fish. Tidal currents make an enormous difference in fishing success near interrupted bottom contours. I choose this spot where the ebbing tidal flow sweeps natural feed along the island's rocky beach and spews it across the sandy bottom. I'm not surprised to see an area of clean sand remains, although it seems somewhat smaller. A seaworm dressed hook immediately brings up a platter-sized flounder. This is enough for dinner, but being a serious fisherman I try for a bigger one. Each larger fish insures release of the preceding one until I'm satisfied I have the best available. I then stitch a doubled piece of marline through the mouth and gill and secure both ends around the starboard riser about midship. Flipping the fish over the rail into the cold water will keep him fresh as I further explore nature's wonders along the shoreline.

In less than two hours I'm back in the cove. I gut the flounder on the edge of the float with my four-inch pocketknife, wishing I had packed my nine-inch filleting tool. Not having the proper cookware, I scrounge several feet of lashing wire I find wrapped around a telephone pole on the cottage road. Necessity being the mother of invention, I crudely skin the flounder's back with my inadequate knife and then wire the fish, belly-side down, against a four-foot piece of pine plank found jammed into the scrub brush. With the head and tail securely wired, several turns are made around the middle to keep the cooked meat from falling into the fire.

An hour before sunset, the roaring fire diminishes to a pile of cherry red embers and I place my unopened can of baked beans against the edge of the glowing mound. An old trick passed down from a boyhood friend requires the can's top and bottom to bulge and return three times, to pressure cook the contents. This method of cooking canned goods was used during camping trips. My instructional friend did get sidetracked once while can-cooking beans on his apartment hot plate. Distracted by a telephone call, he spent a good part of a week cleaning beans and molasses off the ceiling and walls. He never did get all the flattened ones off the ceiling, which were damn near hidden under the fresh coat of paint.

A pedestal consisting of several stones holds my pine plank angled over the hot coals, far enough away to keep the pine from flaming. With the fish wired to the underside, the broiling begins. By the time the bean can bulges and retracts three times, it's ready to open. The fish is also done to perfection. After eating the back, I lift the frame exposing the underside meat, which is just as tasty, but without the crispness. Along with hot beans, a can of warm soda, and wild berries picked from the bushes, the meal is a camping success.

I prepare the tent for my last night and suddenly remember I haven't called my kids.

Mike picks up the phone on the second ring. When I begin to speak, he interrupts, telling me he and his sister received my letters this afternoon and have been trying to reach me for hours.

"Have you gone to the authorities yet?" he asked.

"No," I reply. "Several things have transpired since, and I've been spending a few days at Uncle Lloyd's old cottage in Maine to think things through."

I detect a sigh of relief in his voice. Then he strongly requests me to reconsider informing anyone.

"I spoke to Sally right after receiving your letter. She also got it this afternoon and agrees with me you should leave well enough alone. Please don't do this, for everyone's sake," he continued.

"You know I've been living with this for years, and this decision has developed over a very long time. I'm putting off disclosure until I sort out some relationships that were unexpected."

Mike again implores me to reconsider and elicits my promise to call him before going to the police. I agree, and tell him I'll call his sister right away. He warns me that Sally is pretty hysterical not knowing about this situation earlier and will be extremely agitated when I call her.

He is right. Sally is completely shaken by the whole concept and is unable to understand my not informing them before now. I assure her I'll consider my impending plans and speak with both of them before proceeding. I insist she and Mike not come to New England while I work through this. I now dread they may come, regardless of my demand. I regret not telling them before I left Florida.

With these difficult calls behind me, I prepare to retire for the night. The brilliant dome of blue gradually darkens, and shiny diamonds appear scattered across the heavens. I bed down, expecting a peaceful night, but mentally unsettled by my kids' first reactions to the letter. I'm determined to put these thoughts aside until morning when reality becomes better grounded in the light of day.

Shivering in my skimpy sleeping bag, I awake at dawn to a fresh Nor'wester rattling my tent. The change in temperature doesn't concern me, because I'm leaving the island today.

When I arrive at the ramp looking for a ride ashore, the cove is full of activity, if one can call three boats tied to the float at the same time activity. George Bailey is one of the occupiers, but he is loaded with newly-built pots to be set offshore. I ask the pilot of the empty clinker double-ender if he is going to the mainland, and I'm welcomed aboard as he casts off, maneuvering the craft through the mooring field to the cove's entrance. Bobby's vessel is a converted lifeboat, partially decked, and has a hydraulic pot-hauling slave and davit. He fishes single pots to avoid the dangers of handling trawls while alone. The "clinker" hull construction, also called "lapstrake," appears as clapboards on a house. That is, the planks overlap rather than being joined edge to edge. I hand Bobby a ten and carry my stuff to the car. On reaching U.S.1, I turn southeast and estimate five hours to the motel, including time for a quick lunch.

Once in town, my first stop is at Tommy Phillips' place to drop off four live lobsters brought from Maine. They are surprised and pleased as they crowd them onto the bottom refrigerator shelf. I graciously, I hope, refuse their invitation for a lobster dinner claiming exhaustion, and preferring instead to unwind in my room and contemplate the coming events. Arlene reconfirms tomorrow's dinner arrangements, assuring me Ann is looking forward to the evening.

I'm in my room after first shaking an evening snack from the ornery dispenser outside the manager's office. The day's activities finally overtake me. I land on the bed in a heap. Trying to imagine the multitude of possibilities tomorrow evening may present, I'm out like a doused light.

Four

I oversleep Friday morning. Lying awake and staring at the ceiling, I contemplate what interesting turn the day will bring. Unsure how tonight's dinner will present an opening to advance my association with Ann, I stumble through the day without forming any practical tactics. I wonder if this is how one feels beginning a courtship late in life. I resist thoughts of diminished capacity, believing instead my lack of ideas is due to my absence from the dating scene so many years.

The sun is still high when I arrive at the Phillips' place right on time. I notice a small pale green sedan in the driveway behind Tom's SUV. This may be Ann's car, which proves to be the case. She is waiting for me in the walkway. Together, we climb the porch steps. I can't help but notice she is decked out in a nicely fitted black skirt and ivory-lace top, accentuating her petite figure. I detect a faint hint of the same "Wind Song" aroma in her wake, while she walks ahead of me to the foyer.

"Looks like we're both punctual people," she whispers before announcing our presence.

"Welcome to the house of spirits," announced Tom, who had sneaked up behind us from the adjoining study. "The bar is set up in the end of the dining room around the corner, with enough variety to make one forget about dinner or anything else if you're not careful."

"You know my limit Tommy, just one gin and tonic," Ann replies.

"Make it two," I chime in. "My size allows for a second one, but that's my limit."

"Arlene will be down in a minute. I hope you didn't think I'm mixing these two Manhattans for myself," replied Tom. "So tell us about the trip to your uncle's island in Maine. How long since you've been there?"

"It's been more than forty years at least since I spent summers working away my school vacations. The visit brought back a lot of memories. The place has hardly changed; even the population stays the same. Caught a few fish and slept in a tent for the first time since I can remember. I also had a chance to borrow a dory and skirt the shoreline."

"I love islands. The remoteness and quiet seem like another world. I could live like that forever," Ann replies.

That's nice to hear. Not many women take kindly being cut off from shopping centers and such. She is becoming more interesting every minute. That comment goes in the plus column —so far there have been no minuses.

"Why don't we take these drinks onto the back deck and enjoy the late afternoon sun before leaving for dinner?" suggests Tom. "Bring that basket of cheese and crackers. I'll get the door, Holt. By the way, thanks again for the lobsters. They were delicious."

Arlene appears on deck and the four of us quickly settle in soft-cushioned brightly-colored deck chairs positioned semicircle in front of Tom's recently purchased chiminea. Glowing red coals radiating heat from the ceramic belly warm our legs, negating the evening chill.

Following twenty minutes of small talk, Tom begins the inquiry I had been hoping to avoid since arriving in town.

"So, just what is this old business you came so far to attend to anyway? It must be awfully important to personally come all this way. Couldn't you have taken care of it by mail or something?"

I'd been giving thought to a question like this beforehand,

so I am not taken entirely by surprise.

"Well, as you correctly stated, my business concerns matters that are quite old. I came back to repair an error made a long time ago concerning certain historical presumptions. I can't elaborate more until all the loose ends are attended to, which I expect will be within a few weeks. I apologize for being vague, but please believe me, it's the only way I feel I can bring this to a proper conclusion."

"Wow! I thought you were here only to kick a few tires and get the lay of the town after being away so long. From the sound of it, you're really serious about this. I apologize for prying."

"Think nothing of it. I realize my sudden appearance, after my long absence, invites questions. I'd rather not address them now, but I'll thoroughly explain myself soon."

Arlene quickly offers more cheese and crackers. Attempting to change the subject, she requests that Tom add more wood to the fire. He agrees, but promptly forgets. I redirect the conversation to Ann, a subject I'm most interested in, inquiring how their friendship started.

Ann begins, "Tom brought Arlene to town after they were married and settled near here while Tom's parents were still alive. Arlene and I met at the PTA when our daughters were small. We've been friends ever since. My husband Ed and Tom also got along well, which encouraged the relationship.

"What line of work was your husband in?"

"He graduated from MIT and worked thirty six years for Reese Specialty Valve in Quincy." He passed away three years before he planned to retire.

I express my condolences as best I can, then give Tom a "let's leave look," which he correctly responds to by swallowing the last third of his Manhattan and announces we ought to go soon or we'll miss our reservation. Tom offers to drive, so we all pile into his new SUV and head toward the restaurant. An uneasy feeling comes over me when Tom turns his vehicle onto the local roadway rather than using the parallel highway. This is completely unexpected, for I believe the highway is the shorter route. This road passes Dickey's grave and is the same one I traveled with shovel and hoe the night of his burial.

"Why so quiet in back?" asked Tom, as we approach the grave only I am aware of. "Sorry, just thinking about the pleasant evening we have ahead of us," I answer.

Ann comments, "The Mill House is my favorite local restaurant. We always saved it for special occasions, which made the evening even nicer."

Although she seems to participate in the conversation, I detect Ann is not at all relaxed. She is perched on the edge of the seat. I reach for her hand that's gripping the front seat back. Patting it, I place it in her lap. She smiles and reclines back into her seat.

"I'm leaving you guys out front while I park the car," Tom announces as we arrive at our destination.

He rejoins us shortly, and we step into the tastefully decorated reception area and wait for the hostess. The dining room replicates an eighteenth century colonial inn. Authentic antique desks, ladder-back chairs, armoires, and pine dining tables are discreetly positioned throughout giving intimacy to various dining locations. We are greeted by the pleasant hostess and seated at one of the linen-draped tables across from the fireplace. The room is nearly empty, and quiet enough for easy conversation.

"The town history's latest edition has three photographs of this building—one picture shows it as a working mill, then as it sat idle after World War 2, and then restored and remodeled as it is now," offers Tom.

"I remember when this was a rundown building in the late forties. We used to catch herring by hand during the spring run," I respond. "They would congregate in the pool under the broken waterwheel, before charging up the concrete fish ladder to the pond. Sometimes the catching was so fast we didn't see the warden approaching. He could only grab one or two of us at a time—the rest would scatter. An on-the-spot scolding and a letter to our parents were the only repercussions, so we weren't terribly deterred.

"Did you live over the hill above the pond?" asked Ann.

"That's where I was born and lived my first sixteen years," I replied.

"You must have known my brother, Richard, then. He should be about your age I think."

"Yes, yes, I believe we were in the same class and the same room." I almost add, "About the time he disappeared," but I restrain myself.

I am taken aback by the sudden connection, and more so because of her use of "should be" instead of "would have been." I dare not question this tense, but find it extremely curious, even worrisome. Does Ann think her brother is alive? I now realize I'm completely ignorant of the accepted resolution of Dickey's disappearance.

The waitress approaches our table, squashing the subject. She smiles pleasantly and announces, "We have a nice selection of dinner wines if someone would like to make a choice from our wine list."

Ann and I agree on glasses of house Zinfandel. Tom and Arlene choose a bottle of medium-priced Merlot after some minor dickering about labels.

"If your business in town is going to last much longer, how about staying with us instead of that motel you're camped in?" Tom asks. "We have plenty of room and would be happy for you to stay with us for as long as you want."

Caught off guard, I thank him profusely, but decline by suggesting one of my kids may be joining me soon. "Besides, I or we, may be occupied for some time tying up loose ends," I lied.

Feeling bad that I had refused his offer, I compound it with another subterfuge. "Maybe I'll be able to take you up on your offer after my son leaves."

I really want to be alone, but dare not admit it. Tom says he understands and the conversation changes to the unwelcome changes to the town, which are turning the quiet fishing village into a Boston bedroom community.

Ann asks, "Where have you been eating your meals while you're in town, Holt?"

"Several places here and in the next village. My favorite is the "Copper Bucket" down at the harbor front."

"Why, you must have met my daughter then. She's a waitress at the Bucket."

"Do you mean the pretty blond with the model's walk?" I ask.

"Yes, that's Jenny. Osborne is her married name. You aren't the stranger she spilled the coffee on are you?"

"That I am," I reply.

"Oh, she was so upset and then was flabbergasted by the generous tip you gave her. She couldn't remember if she thanked you."

"She certainly did, as I sloshed my way toward the door. The tip was just a way of helping smooth out what was obviously a trying day for her. Besides, I got two cups of coffee and it didn't cost me a cent."

Our wine arrives, and after Tom's sniffing and swirling, he offers a toast. "To the four of us, old friends, new friends, and a bright future." I wish I knew who nudged my foot during the toast.

With our orders placed, the conversation is interrupted by a boisterous arrival, making his way toward the adjoining lounge. The gentleman stops at our table, loudly greeting my companions. The man's approach appears more like swaggering than a gentleman's walk. Well proportioned and with what looks like a six-and-a-half-foot height, he commands more space than ordinary men. His manner irritates me when we are reintroduced.

"Holt, do you remember Ben Griffin from grade school? Ben, this is Holt Tilden visiting from Florida," Tom announces.

"Hello, Ann, nice to see you this evening. Yes, I remember Holt. We were in the old school building a few years back. What brings you back to town now, may I ask?"

"Just a visit, Ben. It's nice to see you again," I fibbed.

Ben must be a year older than I and was in the class ahead of me in grade school. He was also Dickey's best friend around the time he disappeared. During my remaining few years in town, I avoided him like the plague. He never physically harassed me, but his mean looks and attitude in the hallways gave me shivers, like he wanted to reach out and grab me. I thought if anyone suspected my part in Dickey's demise, it was him.

"You must still live here, Ben," I add, attempting to mask my dislike by offering some conversation.

"I've always been here and plan on staying until they run me out of town."

Turning toward the others he is obviously edging me out of the conversation. Ben compliments Ann's appearance, then follows with more small talk before departing for the bar. He leaves none too soon to suit me. I take some satisfaction in noticing Ann's apparent coolness toward him during the unwelcome interlude.

"He's been divorced ten years or more and is quite the lady's man around town," Tom explains. "I know Ann is on his wish list, much to her disgust." My dislike for Ben Griffin is growing.

After rolls and salads are consumed the main course arrives and well worth the wait. Both the Phillips' have the broiled scrod entrée with something brown and flat that I can't identify. Ann and I have small portions of the broiled scallop casserole. The Scallops were termed "Ipswich" but the waitress divulges they were actually harvested from Cape Cod, not more than seventy miles away and are delivered daily. That's a stretch of "truth in advertising" I think, but there's no question they are delicious.

We finish the meal with sips of Bailey's Irish Cream and leave the establishment nearly three hours later. After more liqueurs at Tom and Arlene's, without Ann's participation, we are both out the door and in the driveway where I extract her cellphone number with little resistance. After an awkward hug, we climb into our respective cars. She enters the street first, and I watch her car's tail lights fade into the still night mist.

As I drive toward the motel, I ask aloud what I am doing. Anticipating the coming days, I wonder where it all will end. This uncertainty is worrisome, but exciting at the same time. Behind it all, I know the time will come when I'll need to tell Ann of my involvement in her brother's disappearance. Right now, I haven't the foggiest idea when, but I know it must be done… and soon.

Five

My head is so full of extraneous ideas that I toss and turn in bed. Irritated, I get up and open the window facing the woods behind my room. I wonder aloud why they keep the heat up so damn high in these rooms all day long. In bed again, sleep eventually overtakes me.

*

It's Saturday and Mike's eighth birthday. I have to leave the kid's party right after it begins. I have critical work to accomplish at the office. Mike cries and pulls at my sleeve when I edge toward the door. I'm soaked in perspiration when I approach the car. All the little party guests rush by me, yelling and crying as they leave for home. Mike stands in the doorway looking so alone. I wave goodbye and drive off.

*

I sit upright in a sweat. The red numerals on the bedside clock indicate two thirty. Only two thirty! I can't believe two hours have passed since I last looked. It's going to be a long night. I try to analyze my nightmare. I never left Mike's birthday party or anything else that I can remember. I fall asleep again and the dreams are almost repeated.

The alarm buzzes. It's seven o'clock. I'm on my feet and halfway into the bathroom, when the night's adventures come to mind. Not one to analyze dreams, this one causes me to wonder if there is significant meaning. I dismiss the thought and prepare for the day.

Driving toward the harbor, I eagerly anticipate seeing Jenny, knowing now that she is Ann's daughter. She seems to be a sweet young woman, a late replica of her mother. I wonder how she will take our association. Jenny eyes me when I enter the restaurant. To my surprise, she ushers me to the table by the window overlooking the harbor and places one of the brand new menus in my hand.

"Mother tells me you both had a wonderful dinner with the Phillips at the Mill House last evening."

I'm surprised and pleased that Ann was eager enough to inform her daughter so soon after the event.

"We did have a nice dinner, and the company was the best around. I only became aware of your relationship to Ann last night. You must have talked to her this morning, I guess."

"Actually she called me last night."

Jenny ends the sentence with no more elaboration. I believe she feels she's volunteered too much already, but I'm happy she's divulged as much as she has, and decide not to question her further.

"Your mother is a wonderful lady. I consider myself fortunate we were introduced by the Phillips."

"Well, you two seem to have hit it off," she offered. "We've missed you here. I understand you've been to Maine."

"Yes, a couple of days to reminisce about childhood vacations on one of the islands."

"That's nice. The usual coffee? What else would you like this morning, Mr. Tilden?"

"Can we dispense with the Mr. Tilden? Holt will be fine."

"Very well, Holt, this just seems a little odd, or I should say, new for me. Mother and I have been especially close since Dad passed three years ago. You're the first man she has ever spoken of favorably since. Oh, my! There I go again."

Seeing her blush, I respond, "Don't worry. I'll never tell. Today I think I'll have two eggs, over medium, hash browns, and wheat toast."

"No bacon?"

"Not today. I love it, but I'm trying to control the fat intake."

"Don't go away, be back in a jiffy. Here's today's paper if you like," she offers, removing one from the vacant table beside me.

On opening the County Ledger, I see most of the front page devoted to the latest scandal. "Retired County Assessor Implicated in Kickback Scheme." Nothing new here, I think, scanning the first few lines. Then, as I prepare to turn the page, Benjamin Griffin's name catches my attention. Reading the entire front and second page article, I discover he is the retired assessor and the individual being investigated! According to the paper, there are documents and depositions backing the charge of him arranging low assessments for a price. I think back to last evening's chance encounter, and his comment, something about staying here until they run him out of town. I am not unhappy about this development.

My meal arrives and I show the front page to Jenny. She glances at it and tells me bits of background regarding Griffin.

"He's been in politics as long as I can remember, and was assessor for ten years or more before retiring a couple of years ago. He sold his surveying company about the time he retired. I shouldn't say this, but Mom dislikes him a lot. Sometimes I think… oh, never mind. I should keep those kinds of things to myself."

"I understand, Jenny. Some people come on too strong, and for whatever reason, we feel they're threatening or undesirable. This is one way we protect ourselves. No need to feel guilty about it."

The breakfast goes down quickly, and I leave after settling the bill and promising to keep this conversation between the two of us.

After leaving, I drive along the harbor front, in time to

fall in behind a lobster-bait truck leaving the town pier. It proceeds to grind its way up the hill ahead of me. Fish juice cascades from under the tail gate onto the road. From the aroma I believe the bait is more than a couple of days old, so I slow down, attempting to avoid rivulets of gurry streaming under the car. The gap between us grows; lessening the stench, part of the fishing village flavor.

Since returning on Thursday from Maine, I've been resisting an urge to visit the roadside grave. I cannot fathom what possible good seeing this would do, but I find myself traveling in that direction.

Brilliant red and yellow maple leaves lay scattered across the roadway, filling both gutters level to the curbing, reminiscent of fifty years ago. I slow to a stop across the street. Residents are at work and children in school. The neighborhood is eerily quiet. I walk across the street and then turn south along the curb, searching for something familiar in the landscape. Not knowing what to look for, I reverse direction and proceed approximately two hundred feet beyond where I think the grave is located. I retrace my steps again. Something doesn't seem right. I study the opposite side of the street. There sits a small Victorian-styled house set back fifty feet from the road. The structure looks unchanged since I was a child. The narrow lot mandates the driveway be sandwiched between the building and the privet hedge on the lot line. I am sure this has never been relocated since it was originally placed, and I now realize this driveway is directly across the street from where I dug the hole.

Of all places to build! Across the street from the driveway is a concrete apron and dirt road leading to another house built in the very woods I used for cover as a boy. I feel certain that within eight or ten feet north or south, lies Dickey's grave. I wonder if the workmen will cut through the apron or avoid it. The terrain behind the sidewalk is overgrown with enormous trees and underbrush except the small area near the building. Concrete on each side of the apron is severely heaved from tree roots, elevating some areas as much as five inches. My thoughts return to last evening, when we approached this from the north. The demolition crew had already torn up the old walk and installed new forms halfway to here. I'm guessing they'll be working this area in another three weeks.

Six

After returning to my room, I place a call to Ann. She sounds breathless when answering the phone on the third ring.

"Ann, this is Holt. Have you anything planned this evening? If not, how about we attend the Autumn Festival at the harbor and then get something to eat?"

"I'd love to go. Thank you for asking. When would you like to leave?"

"Is four o'clock too early for you?"

"Not at all. I'll be ready. Is there anything I should bring other than myself?"

"Just dress casual. Bring along something warm for after the sun sets—might get a little chilly down there."

It's nearly lunch time, so I grab a couple of items from the vending machines and climb into my car. I have several hours before picking up Ann, so decide to visit Alden. I feel sorry he is in such serious condition and think a visit might do some good. We spent so much time together as kids, I wouldn't feel right not seeing him again.

We called him "Huck." A lanky loose-limbed teenager with an inquiring mind, an inventor's heart, and contrarian nature, he was my best friend. We agreed on many things and fiercely fought over the rest. We were woodsmen, mechanics, inventors, divers, campers, and boaters. I'm told he last earned his keep consulting for various electronic laboratories along Route 128.

Traveling west on Bay Hill Road, I cross the highway and turn into Alden's yard. Both the vehicles under the oak tree are in the same location and condition as before. There's a space for me to park behind the pickup. I cross the unmowed lawn and climb the long flight of stairs to a decrepit porch and rim-racked screen door. I judge a knock here will be useless, so I pull the flimsy thing open and reach for the house door, giving it another firm rap. With no response again, I pound the door and loudly announce my name.

"It's open, come on in," Alden faintly calls from a distance.

To get the wooden door open, requires moving two cardboard boxes full of junk that's blocking access. For that matter, most of the ten-by-twenty foot porch is littered with boxes of what looks to contain trash.

"Are you in here Alden? It's Holt. I came to visit if you'd like."

"I'm in the kitchen. You can find your way through the dining room."

The house is in shambles. Never have I seen such clutter and trash inside anyone's home. Remembering the house when we were children, being clean and well kept as my own, I am shocked by the change. Alden sits alone in the kitchen in some sort of recliner covered with various dirty blankets, towels, and newspapers wrapped around and underneath him. The room temperature is as cold as the outside air, around sixty degrees. A small portable television occupies the counter next to the sink, with an old black and white movie flickering without sound. He directs me to sit in a little-used guest chair, loaded with stacks of newspapers and magazines. I remove the pile and sit down.

"How are you feeling today?" I hated to ask.

"I feel like I look, and that's damn bad, Hoot."

I am surprised he revived my old nickname.

Alden continued, "Doc keeps me drugged so damn much, can't even tell what day it is."

I'm here to cheer him up, but he isn't going to make it easy. For whatever reason, I begin to tell him of my earlier visit to the Pit, but avoid the part about finding Pup's marker.

"I ain't been down that road in twenty years. That was the best time of my life. It's been straight downhill ever since. Wife ran off leaving me a no-good son, not even sure he's really mine. He can't even take care of the place."

We reminisce about some of the good times camping in the remote wilderness a half mile from home. I see a weak smile and moist eyes as he recalls things I can't even remember. I try to prolong the subject, but the thread is lost and the spark dies.

I observe the desperate surroundings. Dirty dishes fill the sink, more precariously stacked on the counters. Filthy windows stare back between tattered curtains. Gravity hugs everything spilled on the worn linoleum-covered floor. The home reeks of failure, neglect and depression. I see only remorse in his eyes, his painful life wasting away, wishing for its final breath.

I leave Alden's place feeling damn low. What an awful existence. I've seen misery before, but have difficulty purging his prognosis from my mind until I drive over a gray squirrel. He thumps and bumps under the car. I see in the mirror his mangled body spinning off the road behind me. Reality regained —no one is immune to misfortune.

Once in my room, I prepare for the evening. At 3:45 I leave for Ann's home, consulting the neatly written directions she handed me the day before. During the drive, thoughts of Ann's earlier life with a loving husband and delightful daughter come to mind. I feel like a trespasser, invading another man's territory. My "life must go on" attitude is tested.

As I approach the address I'm pleased to find a well-manicured landscape, complementing an immaculate white cape dwelling atop a small hill. Slowing to stop beside her car, she appears from behind the house to greet me. With her is a rambunctious golden cocker spaniel, apparently returning from a walk. I meet Dixie, and she accepts my presence without alarm. I think it's a good omen to be liked by someone's dog, especially if the animal belongs to a lovely lady.

"You're ten minutes early, enough time for me to show you the house if you like."

"I'd be delighted to see it. You have such a beautiful yard. Do you have a maintenance service?"

"Just the grass, I do the gardens and the inside myself. Gardening is my relaxation— the inside is work."

As we enter, Dixie makes a dash for the water dish nearly tripping me in the hallway. I recover and follow Ann through the house. Warm and inviting, each room is attractively furnished with early American antiques. There is much to admire, including her provocative perfume, which I dare not mention. There are family pictures displayed on the mantle. I learn two of them are of her deceased husband Ed. The first one must have been taken during college, with him in full football gear. The second, of a distinguished middle aged gentleman wearing a McGregor plaid shirt and standing next to a red Corvette on the front lawn. There is also a framed color photograph of Jenny and her husband taken on their wedding day. Ann's picture rests on an antique dry sink near the mantle. I comment on the handsome family pictures and express where I believe Jenny gets her beauty. Ann waves off the compliment with an endearing blush as we ready to leave.

"Be a good girl, Dixie. I'm ready to go if you like."

I hold the door as she enters the car. This is a new aroma. It's certainly not overpowering, more subtle and magnetic. I must ask her about the formula after I get to know her better.

We arrive at the harbor and park behind the bank building on Front Street near the end of the cove. The fair has been in progress most of the day and will end at ten o'clock this evening. The town closes off the entire length of the street two weekends after Labor Day every year for the fall celebration. Art and craft tables and public service booths are crowded along both sidewalks in front of the stores. Various music groups command the three intersections where roads from the hillside meet Front Street. Carnival rides for the kids occupy half the parking lot behind the stores.

"How about walking north on this side and returning on the opposite one," I suggest.

"Fine with me. It looks like most of the town decided to come here at the same time, doesn't it?"

"Ann, Ann," we hear from a female voice across the street. "Over here," she yells, while waving a gold-colored bag in her right hand.

"Doris," replies Ann as we meet in the middle of the street. "What ever do you have in the bag?"

"I couldn't help myself. I bought this wonderful hand-knit Christmas scarf for my daughter in Idaho."

"Why, it's exquisite, Doris. I'd like you to meet my friend, Holt Tilden, all the way from Florida. Holt lived here when he was a boy."

"It's nice to meet you Holt—do you come back to town often"?

"Nice meeting you also, Doris. No, this is a special trip, to get reacquainted with the town."

"Well, you picked the right season. The colors this year are splendid, don't you think?"

"Indeed they are. Last week must have been the peak."

Turning to Ann, Doris mockingly asked, "How long have you been keeping this man hidden from us?"

"What a thing to say. Obviously if he were hidden, he wouldn't be standing here now, would he?" replies Ann.

"I'm only joking. I didn't mean to imply you were really keeping him hidden."

"I know you didn't—I was just ribbing you back for once."

After a few minutes of conversation, we leave the lady and continue on our way, browsing through the assorted handicrafts. I notice Doris eyeing the two of us from across the street, and I can almost see the wheels spinning inside her head, wondering how much Ann has really been hiding.

When the sun begins slipping below the tree line, folks start donning heavier clothing. Ann unties the thick white sweater from around her waist and slips it over her head. She then pulls it all the way down to her hips.

"That ought to keep you toasty," I comment.

"I've had this sweater for years—it's my most used piece of clothing in the fall."

"You fill it out nicely," I blurt out before thinking.

"Well, thank you. Flattery is scarce at my age."

"I can't believe that," I respond, then decide to abandon the subject before I get in deeper. She buys a few homemade preserves from one of the tables, and we casually stroll among the artist's offerings hanging from skimpy panels behind their booths. The density of people and associated noise dampens our desire to continue, so we agree to duck into her favorite pizza shop at the next intersection.

"Do you come here often?" I inquire.

"I may buy a take-out once a month. I'm sure they have the most delicious pizzas in town."

On entering the shop I see only five tables, three of them already occupied by hungry pizza lovers devouring assorted pies. We decide to share a medium pepperoni, double cheese, bread sticks, and iced tea. While Ann chatters on about her involvement with the local art society, I can't help but study more closely her exquisite features, illuminated by brilliant fluorescent lie detectors hanging from the ceiling. I mentally run the numbers again. She must have been in the third grade, three years behind me in school. That would make her about sixty, and she doesn't look a day over fifty. As I examine everything about her, I'm suddenly aware of a vaguely familiar face peering through the store's front window directly behind her. When our eyes meet, he disappears. For a few moments the encounter is a mystery, and then I realize it was Ben Griffin. This is the second time I've noticed him watching us since we met at the restaurant. I can't help wonder if his appearance here was accidental.

There are no other cars when we pull into the small parking lot above Minot beach. The lot has spaces for four vehicles. The front and sides are hemmed with thick granite curb-stones. Beds of Rosa rugosa contain the lot on three sides. Small waves roll rhythmically across the shallow sand, eventually curling and breaking as they flop onto the beach. Sparkles of moonlight dance intermittently on the surf while broken cumulus clouds drift overhead. I wouldn't be as presumptuous to park here unless agreement had been granted beforehand.

"Want to tell me what you're thinking?" I inquire.

"Just that it's a perfect evening and thank you for asking me out."

"I can't think of anything I'd rather be doing than keeping company with you. It's hard to believe only two weeks ago we met at Tom and Arlene's. I've thought about you constantly since then."

"I've thought a lot about you also, even wondering if I had scared you off when you suddenly left for Maine last week."

Listening to her response, I wonder if Ben Griffin's face in the window confirms his interest like Tom indicated at the Mill House. I can't decide if he is going to be a minor nuisance, or if it's something more serious. We spend the late evening exchanging family histories, sharing some of our most inner thoughts, and marveling at the combined magic of the moon and ocean. I have so much to tell her, but I keep delaying the inevitable, reluctant to break the spell.

For the next several weeks we share some portion of every day. Time apart drags slowly, and when we are together, it's like traveling on an exciting journey, but with my gas gauge on empty. With a little research I find what I anticipate to be an excellent dining place to celebrate our six-week anniversary. I pick up Ann at seven and drive several towns westward, to reach a recently-opened, exclusive eatery that specializes in "Rare Foods and Privacy Well Done." The right parking lot is designated for patrons only. I notice the staff lot on the opposite side.

The restaurant structure is a 150-year-old renovated barn, with enough money spent on improvements inside to construct several million-dollar homes. Inside, all sizes of discretely hidden tables are individually tucked around every corner, including in the original horse stalls. We are encouraged to select a table from the location map over the reception desk. Actually a decorator's plan, the map displays every table's location, including privacy walls and adornments. Available tables are illuminated, with darkened spaces indicating ones already reserved. We make our selection and are ushered to the far side of the building, where we find our cozy table for two surrounded by brilliantly colored orchids, bromeliads, ferns, and other tropicals. The flowers are arranged in tiers and are constantly bathed in thin clouds of water vapor, generating a steamy jungle effect and providing privacy from areas not secluded by walls.

*

With his engine off, Ben Griffin settles into his seat for a long wait. He arrived slightly behind Holt's car and parked unnoticed on the far edge of the lot. Ben has been watching Ann's house for days, expecting to find them together sooner or later. He's often thought of Holt Tilden and unexpectedly meeting him at the Mill House rekindled those memories. His friend Baxter, that snitch, frequents his thoughts also. The two men are forever woven into the fabric of his life. Never imagining Holt would return to town, he's rankled at seeing him making a play for his Ann. "Well, not if I have anything to say about it. I've waited too long. Now it's my turn," he thought.

*

Ann has been speechless walking from the reception desk to the table. If I hadn't taken her hand, I'm sure she would have wandered off. I couldn't break the silence as we traveled through the opulence, taking it all in.

"Do you think we can find something to eat in here?" I ask, as we are seated at the table.

"We don't need food to appreciate the décor, but I'm sure we'll be satisfied with whatever we have," she replies.

We decide on a light Mateus Rosé wine, which is delivered after receiving the voluminous menu, listing meat dishes from roast Australian lamb to Peking duck and most of the edible fish swimming the oceans.

"I can't believe this place," she exclaims. "How did you ever find it?"

"By doing a little research," I reply. "It is a little fancy, isn't it? You know something else? They expect to serve each table only once each evening, so the guests have it for the entire night if they wish. By the way, they close at 2:00 a.m., so we have plenty of time."

Ann looks at me as if I were a complete mystery, which of course is truer than she knows.

"Have you seen anything you like on the menu?" I ask.

"The Caesar salad is always nice, but way too much for me to eat before a meal."

"How about we split one? That way, I'll save room for whatever comes next," I suggest.

"I was hoping you would say that. For the main course, I'm thinking of something in the fish department. Seafood is my favorite, both fin and shellfish. I haven't figured which of these exotic preparations I'll try."

"Fish is my favorite too. I love swordfish, and unless the waiter recommends a better alternative, that's what I'm having."

The impeccably tailored attendant, still bronzed from the late summer sun and wearing white cotton gloves, arrives to receive our order. We are to call him Jonathan. After conveying the offered specialties, he recites Ann's request, "potato crusted halibut with smoked haddock custard and Irish buttered sauce." He does the same with my fresh swordfish steak, "grilled to achieve perfect texture and moistness, served with my choice of fresh peas, a loaded baked potato, and apple crisp." Two tall candles, mounted in polished brass holders, are retrieved from one of the planters. They are lighted and placed at each end of our flowering centerpiece, before Jonathon backs away from the table and silently leaves.

"This is really too extravagant," exclaims Ann.

"I should tell you that I never dine this way myself, but I thought it would be a unique experience for both of us."

"Well, now I am disappointed. I thought you always dined this opulently."

"It's nice to see you have a sense of humor," I respond.

"Jenny tells me you had breakfast at the Bucket this morning. She even told me what you ate."

"I can see I'll have to watch what I say, or at least measure my words."

"She is very protective, especially since her dad passed away. She's also discrete and usually guarded, unless she feels she's with friends. I only hope she never misjudges one for the other. I worry about her being too trusting."

"I think you have a delightful daughter. She radiates enthusiasm and character like her mother. She also appears cool-headed and responsible. I wouldn't worry about her too much."

After an appropriate amount of time, our waiter and his assistant arrive bearing our dinners. They position themselves behind us and both dinners contact our table at precisely the same moment. Jonathan inquires if everything is satisfactory— we answer in the affirmative. He leaves an electronic signaling device to use when service is again needed. Both servers back away from the table in unison and disappear. Ann is impressed.

Finishing the meal with crème brulee and caffeine-free coffee lubricate two hours of conversation, where we exchange more details of our former lives. I notice she never reveals anything about the years between her brother's disappearance and her progression through grade and high school. I choose not to inquire about this, as it could dampen an otherwise delightful evening.

We leave the restaurant after midnight. Most of the diners have already departed. There are four vehicles, including mine, in the patron parking lot. As we pull into the street, a dark Ford pickup comes to life from the far end of the lot and quickly enters the lane behind us. Peering into my rear view mirror, I detect only one occupant. I find this curious and casually mention it to Ann. She turns quickly to see for herself, but it's too late. We are already accelerating, and the distance between us has widened. Ann appears restless, and I inquire if something is bothering her.

"No, I'm fine."

"Great, I think we should take the scenic way home if you don't object."

"Sounds good to me. I like the river road through the sanctuary."

My idea is to make several turns after leaving the highway and then pull into a residential driveway, under the guise of checking one of the front tires. After stopping, I take my time at the front wheel, allowing a couple of cars to pass, but no black truck appears. I wonder if this may have been Griffin again. I drive, again with her concurrence, to Minot Beach, a place where we never seem to be disturbed. I have so much I'd like to tell her, but I'm unsure when, or in what order I should proceed. I decide to explore her thoughts on Ben Griffin.

"Do you ever think you are being followed?"

Her eyes reveal total surprise, and her response presents an opening I neither expected nor am I prepared.

"I used to, but not so much now. When my brother first

vanished, I was certain he had run away. The official case has never been solved, but I still believe he decided to leave and is living somewhere nearby."

Stunned, I could only muster, "Why would you think that?"

"I've never told anyone except my husband about this, not even Jenny or Arlene. On the day Richard disappeared, he knew I was going to tell our parents about the abuse he'd been inflicting on me for over a year. He'd already left for school when I told them, and they made me stay home that day. Mom and Dad had no idea what had been going on, and they couldn't understand how it could have happened without them knowing. Richard was in deep trouble, and he knew it. He never returned home that afternoon, and I believe he ran away to escape punishment. For years afterward, I caught glimpses of him, usually in crowds mixed in with strangers. It hasn't happened so much lately. I wonder now if it was my imagination, or if he was actually watching me."

I feel torn with guilt at not divulging my involvement from the beginning. What a damn shame this nightmare has plagued her so long and I'm wholly to blame. I know I must level with her without further delay, even though this moonlit beach is not the setting I would have chosen. What possible excuse could justify prolonging my silence? Her faraway look diminishes, and she seems completely focused as I begin.

"I'm so sorry you had all these years of anguish and uncertainty. You can't imagine how heavily this weighs on me. I've been so captivated by your company since arriving in town I've neglected the very reason for coming back."

She seems to be holding her breath. I reach for her hand and continue.

"I'll get to the point without dragging this out. I was in the sixth grade with your brother. He also bullied me when no one in authority was watching. One afternoon he caught me in the woods while I was walking home from school. When I

realized he was approaching, I grabbed the metal rod I'd kept in
my school bag for protection. When he rushed me from behind,
I struck him once in the head. Not knowing he was seriously
hurt, I went to school the next day and found the police asking
questions regarding his whereabouts. I was scared. I know I
should have told the authorities right away, but I didn't."

Ann's sobbing interrupts my monologue. Risking
rejection, I move my right hand to her shoulder. She doesn't
resist, as her head drops forward. Her eyes squint, as glistening
tears stream down her face.

I force myself to continue. "I buried Richard near where
he fell and never told anyone. My reason for returning is to
finally admit everything to the police and hopefully close the
book before I die. I never dreamed we would meet and be
joined together in such a tragic circumstance."

I realize my teeth are chattering and my whole body is
shaking. I try to subdue the tremors. Ann is full-out crying. I
extend my arm around her shoulders. She turns toward me, tears
flooding my neck and collar. I beg her forgiveness. She nods her
head in the affirmative, but the tears continue. I wonder how
many will fall before she requires a drink of water. Annoyed by
the thought, I realize extreme tension can trigger ridiculous
visions. No doubt, I am tense tonight.

"Do you want to go home?" I ask.

I sense her head shaking, which I interpret as yes, so
patting her knee, I start the car and enter the road. In her
driveway I'm unsure whether to leave the engine going or
switch it off. With it still running, she gives me a quick kiss on
my still damp neck, and is out the door.

*

An hour earlier, Ben was pounding both fists on his
steering wheel. Damn it to hell, how could I have lost them, he
shouted at the windshield. Infuriated, he drove directly to Ann's
street and parked off the pavement several houses away from
hers. After cooling down a few minutes, he realized he would be

easily seen when they return. The hell with this, he shouted as he stomped the accelerator to the floor. One tire squealed, then another, as they contacted macadam.

*

I'm spent by the time I arrive at the motel. Lying awake, I speculate what might be coming next. Ann seems to have accepted my revelation without obvious animosity. I wonder how she will handle this over time. Contemplating an uncertain future, I fall asleep, only to be awakened by the cell phone ringing in my pants pocket. I stumble over shoes, scrambling for my clothes in the dark— I'm too late. It's two thirty. I've been in bed only an hour. Seeing Ann's number on the display, I return the call.

"Will you come over?" she asks.

The garage door is up when I arrive. Her car is parked on one side leaving room for me to park. I exit my vehicle. The motor groans as the garage door rumbles down the tracks. An overhead light doesn't come on with the door energized. Had she loosened the bulb? Ann stands in the doorway leading to the kitchen. She's wearing some sort of nightwear. The dim backlight reveals her delicate profile. Unable to summon the appropriate words, I enter the hall and hold her in my arms. With her head on my chest, we continue the embrace and crab our way to the living room sofa. Few words are exchanged before we are both asleep.

Seven

Jimmy Evan arrives home at one thirty that same morning. He'd spent the evening again with his buddies Josh and Andy at the highway gin mill, throwing darts and soaking up beer. Today is Jim's thirty-fifth birthday, and no one's even noticed. Not that he cares. Every day is pretty much the same for him, and today is no different. Since his mom left, he and his dad haven't celebrated birthdays or any other holidays for that matter. He has only vague memories of his mother, who walked away the day after his fifth birthday party. This is the only birthday he remembers as a child, and the details, however distorted, still remain lodged in his brain. Other perceptions seem real, but are, for the most part, conjured up from old photographs found in the attic when he was ten. His dad never talked about her, never even told him why she left or where she went. Jim hates his mom for leaving, hates not knowing what happened. He often wonders if they will ever meet. When he was little, he had reoccurring dreams of her return. The reunion would be all tears, hugs, and music, and would take place in the summertime. Thoughts of meeting his mother now are not so grand. Resentment grows deeper each passing year. There are no other women in Jimmy's life now, none that are important anyway. There's Sally down at the West End. She's anybody's girl, anyone who will buy her a couple of drinks and lie to her, has her for the night. This is good enough for him. He hasn't thought about his life beyond that.

Jim works as an oiler for Esposito's Crane Service Company in Brighton. This is the ninth job he's had in the last ten years, and he thinks this one suits him just fine. Union rules mandate an oiler accompany every mobile crane, whether there is actual work for him or not. He has to hustle, sometimes while rigging out the big booms, but preparing the small hydraulic rigs requires very little work. Practically all he has to do is show up at the site. This is the easiest job he has ever had, and he plans to damn well keep it.

This night was no different from any other he thinks, while he climbs the stairs to the porch. Pushing the front door open, he notices the kitchen light reflecting in the dining room window. Aware of the old man's frugality, he wonders why the light is still on. As he rounds the corner, the pungent smell of feces slows his pace. Once through the doorway, he stops, studying the scene before him. His dad looks like he'd slid out of his seat, assuming a sitting position on the floor, with his back supported by the footrest. The chair is jammed against the outside wall. One of the blankets remains partially covering his legs and midsection, the others scattered nearby. Nauseated, Jim stands silently taking in the scene. This could be it. He moves closer and pulls away part of the blanket, revealing small blood stains on his dad's shirt. Pulling the material further uncovers volumes of blood soaking his dad's torso and collecting on the floor. He recoils against the wall. Glancing around the room, he sees blood splattered from ceiling to floor on the wall behind him. Then he notices the butt of his dad's shotgun poking out from under the rags covering his legs.

Back in the dining room, Jim drops into one of the chairs. The stench and blood in the kitchen gags him. With his right foot, he kicks the kitchen door closed with a slam. In the dead silent house, he feels alone for the first time. Thoughts of being rid of the old man after a few days of unpleasantness tend to counter his disgust. He contemplates calling the cops and following whatever procedure they advise. Then a new idea emerges. He wonders if he can get away with hiding the body and cashing his dad's Social Security checks. Two gongs chime from the mantle clock. He decides to put off calling anyone until daylight, giving him more time to consider his options.

With little sleep, Jim is up at dawn. Avoiding the kitchen, he descends the back stairs onto the lawn, where he paces between the house and shed. All the lost sleep trying to figure out his next step was a waste of time. He's no further ahead now than last night. Without focusing on any particular thought, he scans the grounds behind the house, then enters the shed, and stares at the loosely planked floor. He wonders if this could be a safe place to bury the body. Imagining himself moving and burying his dad brings back the nausea he experienced earlier. He returns to the house and dials the police.

An hour passes before two uniformed officers arrive. Jim is standing in the overgrown weeds out front when they pull their unmarked sedan into the driveway. Explaining that the county coroner will be joining them in twenty minutes, they offer their condolences and begin asking questions regarding his dad's recent mental state. The youngest officer takes detailed notes, while his senior, the lieutenant, asks the questions. The coroner arrives on schedule, and the party of four enters the house. Jim is directed to remain in the dining room. When the three officials move into the kitchen, he is aware of photographs being taken, as each camera flash reflects under the closed door. The officer's radios chatter with constant traffic too muffled for Jim to discern the subject or to know if they concern him. A gentle knock at the screen door announces the arrival of Janet Parker, the citizen's advocate he'd been informed was coming. She expresses sympathies and offers to provide additional help if required. Before leaving, she assists Jim with the selection of a funeral home. Two hours later, an ambulance departs for the selected undertaker.

"May we move into your living room? We have a few more things to go over before leaving," the lieutenant requests.

Both officers sit on the sofa, and Jim positions himself in the wooden captain's chair at the end of the coffee table.

"I'm sure you're aware your dad's death was likely caused by injuries sustained by the shotgun. From our observations, the injury may have been self-inflicted. Had your dad ever indicated he might attempt this?"

"That's all he talked about for the last two years. You can ask his doctor or any of his friends about that. He was very sick —he had cancer and it was slowly killing him, you know."

"I understand. It must have been very difficult for your dad and for you also. Now, according to our records, you called the station at 8:11 this morning. Is this when you discovered the body?"

"No, I found him after midnight when I came home. It must have been one or two o'clock."

"Why did you wait until after eight to call us?"

"I don't know. He was dead when I came home and it was real late. I didn't want to bother anyone until morning I guess."

"What did you do between the time you found him and when you called us?"

"I tried to get some sleep."

"Get any?"

"A little."

"Well, for your information, the station is open twenty-four hours a day, every day, all year long, and situations like this should be reported as soon as possible."

"Am I in trouble?"

"No, but we may want to gather more information from you later. You aren't planning on going out of town for a while, are you?"

"Just to work and around here."

"We've got your work address and phone numbers. We'll call you if we need anything. By the way, did Mrs. Wilson give you the numbers of some home cleaning companies?"

"Yeah, I got em."

As the police drive away, Jim is relieved he hadn't tried to hide his dad's body. At the same time, he worries about what may come later.

Eight

I awake with a jolt and visualize broken glass on the floor somewhere near. When I push my body erect on the same sofa we fell into last night, the evening's astonishing turn of events flood my mind. Ann peeks out from the kitchen to see if the shattering glass has aroused her guest.

"So, I woke you?"

"I should have been up by now anyway. What was that terrible crash?"

"I was unloading the dishwasher and one of my best wine glasses hit the floor."

"Sorry about that," I offer while entering the kitchen. "Here let me clean this up."

As I bend to the floor, the aroma of frying maple-cured bacon arouses my appetite. She stands by the sink, washed and ready for the day. Fresh as a daisy comes to mind.

"I've placed guest towels and a safety razor in the first floor lavatory."

"Thanks. Now where would you like me to put this broken glass?"

"Put it in the blue basket under the sink if you will. Sorry I'm so clumsy. My mind must be somewhere else this morning."

"Indeed, we covered a lot of ground yesterday. I can't imagine the shock you must have felt last night. I wish there had been an easy way to convey this bizarre history, but try as I might to soften it, I always came back to simply pouring it out when the opportunity presented itself. Your call, after I went to bed last night, sent me into such a spin I forgot to bring anything with me. The tone of your voice put at rest the thought I might be met with a gunshot."

"That would never happen. Your many years of anguish have been more than matched by my own. What strange scars we must have. Let's be happy we've come this far. I don't want to think about anything but us for a while."

"Good idea. I'm going to get cleaned up before breakfast is ready."

The small lavatory is equipped with everything necessary to begin the day. While shaving, I wonder if the time is right to suggest spending a couple of days camping on Cliff Island. This may appear too committal this early, so I consider carefully sampling the subject before suggesting the trip. When I'm finished, I hear Ann answer her phone on the third ring.

"Ann, its Tommy. I have terrible news about Alden. He passed away last night."

Witnessing her anxiety, I take the receiver and ask for details.

"Sorry to start the day with bad news, Holt, but Bob Jackson from the station called minutes ago with the news. Alden apparently shot himself last night. His boy discovered him and called the authorities early this morning. The body's been taken to Nickerson's Funeral Home."

"That's not surprising to me, considering the condition he's been in. Thanks for letting us know, Tom. I'll stop by the funeral home and ask if they need help on the arrangements. Do you know his son?"

"Not personally. I only know who he is on the street."

"OK, I'll call you back after visiting Nickerson's."

Hanging up the receiver, I take a chair at the breakfast table, trying to plan the day around Alden's death.

Ann sighs. "Poor Alden. He suffered so long he couldn't stand living that way another day I guess. I'll go to the funeral home with you if you'd like."

"Thanks. Do you know anyone at Nickerson's?"

"Yes. They're the only place in town. We used them for Eddy, and they treated us well. Now I hope you're ready for breakfast. I've held the scrambled eggs over, but I think they are still ok."

"Great. Let's eat."

Having breakfast across from Ann, I can hardly grasp the reality of the last six weeks.

My impulsive side kicking in, I decide the time is right and suggest a trip to the island without mentioning the surprise. (So much for sampling the subject beforehand.) She agrees with enthusiasm. We plan on leaving the day after Alden's service.

On the way to the funeral home I pass the sidewalk construction, checking the crew's progress. They are getting close to the grave, but I think we might have another week before they get to the remains. Ann looks straight ahead, oblivious to her brother's location. I would never offer this information and feel certain she will not inquire. It suddenly occurs to me that I haven't thought about going to the authorities for weeks. Certainly my plans have lost steam since meeting Ann. Believing she wouldn't want to reopen the publicity; I decide to carefully word my question.

"Would you rather I not confess my involvement with your brother to the police?"

"That's entirely your decision. It's the reason you came here, and I have no business influencing you one way or another."

"But my question is, do you have a preference?"

"I prefer you make the choice."

"Very well then. I've decided not to proceed. I think it's the best decision for both of us. I'd rather spend energy furthering our relationship and leave the ugly past behind for good."

"That's my desire, too," she replies, quietly exhaling a

long breath.

Jeremiah Nickerson's handshake was as limp as rockweed at low tide. Surprisingly, he had already processed Alden's paperwork and arrangements by the time we arrived.

"The wake will be held Thursday evening at six thirty, with the funeral the following morning at ten," he announces.

"Have arrangements been made regarding payment for your services?" I ask.

"Yes, they have. Mr. Evan's son James has assumed full financial responsibility."

"Are there any relatives to be informed?"

"As I understand it, there are no living relatives except James' estranged mother. There's no requirement she be notified because they are legally separated and James wishes to leave it that way."

It's almost noon. Satisfied Alden's final business is under control, we drive to the harbor for lunch at the Bucket. Jenny is not surprised to see us. I believe she is not surprised at anything about us.

"Ben Griffin went out the back door when you two came in the front, Mom. I'm sure he saw you pass the window on your way to the door! Has he been bothering you again, Mom?"

"Don't you worry about it, dear. He's a little strange, especially since the law seems to be closing in on him."

"He gives me the willies, Mom. Hi Mr. Tilden, I mean Holt."

"Hello again, Jenny," I said, giving her a little sideways hug.

"I don't think he's going to be in town much longer, considering the charges he's up against," Ann said. "He'll be put away for some time if he doesn't leave town before the trial. Either way, it's going to be a life-changing event, and nobody around here will miss him much."

"You guys going to have lunch?" Jenny inquires as we seat ourselves.

"That's why we're here, Miss; what's on the menu today?"

"I think the baked scrod disappeared with the twelve o'clock crowd. We still have freshly made lasagna along with most of the other selections on the menu."

"Lasagna sounds good to me, with ice tea," requests Ann.

"I'll have the same."

"Coming right up. Here's today's paper if you want it," scooping the "Ledger" off the next table, and placing it between us.

The exchange over Ben Griffin clouds my consciousness while we otherwise converse over lunch. He seems to be always on the periphery, everywhere we go. I wonder if it's time to do some sleuthing on my own, or just confront him directly. Whatever I decide, I'll attempt to keep Ann in the dark to lessen her worry.

Alden's wake on Thursday comes soon enough. A big surprise is James' disheveled appearance. Many attendees are in suits, others are dressed casually, but James stands by the closed casket in shop worn jeans and a rock festival tee shirt, bearing hideous images of *skeletons*. This raises more than a few eyebrows around the room. I later find that the funeral director offered the boy one of his jackets to cover the tee shirt, but it was refused. This apparent disrespect doesn't square in my own mind with James settling the entire funeral expense in advance in cash.

Bracing for more of the same, we are satisfied with his attire for the graveside service the following morning. James appears wearing a gray suit, at least one size too small—probably borrowed, considering the ill fit. His new-found appropriateness tempers everyone's disgust of the previous day.

"I'm ready for that island in Maine," Ann whispered as we leave the cemetery.

Nine

Without Ann's knowledge, I've done extensive groundwork regarding the cottage on Cliff Island. My offer to purchase has been accepted, and the owner is holding my deposit, anticipating the closing on the twentieth of November, two weeks away. It only took a phone call to get permission to use the property for a few days. I witness a slight elevation in Jenny's eyebrows when informed of our plans—they quickly come down as she peppers me with questions about the island.

Intermittent shafts of sunlight stab through broken clouds when we arrive at the landing by mid-afternoon. No boats are in view, and I wonder aloud if we can hitch a ride to the island this late in the day. A crisp nor'west breeze chills our backsides while we stomp our feet on the dock and scan the shoreline for signs of activity.

"Let's give it another ten minutes and we'll go over to the River House to see if they can put us up. Leaf peepers ought to be gone by now."

"There's a boat coming around the bend, and it looks like he's heading this way," Ann exclaims.

"You folks look'n for a ride to the island?" inquires the pilot as he nears the float.

"We sure are mister; will you take us?"

"The name's Edward Johansson. Winter rates are thirty-five bucks for the boat each way; here's my card with the cell number. Call anytime, seven to seven. Special rates for off hours.

Climb aboard. All this gear yours?"

"Yeah, we travel pretty heavy, Edward."

"Not many folks going to Cliff this time of year. Don't let the calm fool ya. Gonna come in nor'east later in the week."

Icy tears stream across our faces, as the 150 Yamaha drives the flat-bottomed skiff through cold green water. Minutes later we enter the cove and unload our equipment on the float. No greeting representative occupies the head of the ramp this time. Our pilot explains, that for several years, folks have given up wintering over like they used to. We carry our luggage, including the tent, to my earlier campsite on the cottage lawn. I'd previously prepared Ann for camping, which was indeed a possibility if the building's interior condition failed to meet the cleanliness claimed. All that worry for naught. The rooms, when I peer through the window, are better than advertised—"move in ready" as they say.

"We can't go in there!" exclaims Ann, when I reach for the hidden key over a window and unlock the front door.

"Didn't I tell you I bought it?"

"You didn't!"

Her excited expression reveals her statement is false.

"How do you like it?" I ask, while thumping the outer walls here and there for soundness.

"It's just like you described, view and all. I love it! When did you buy it? Why didn't you tell me before?"

"I did it all by phone, direct with the owner over the last month. I wanted it to be a surprise and wasn't sure how to get you up here. The events of the last several days pushed it along. By the way, I don't own it until the fifteenth, so be careful not to break anything."

"And you brought the tent all the way here to fool me into thinking we were going to actually camp?"

"Of course. It was part of the surprise. Let's check out the rest of the house before it gets dark."

"Where do our lights come from?" she inquires.

"You mean where does the power to light them come from? For tonight we use kerosene in the lamps stored in the hall closet. Tomorrow, I'll look into getting the diesel generator running sometime in the afternoon for hot water, lights, and appliances. The stove and refrigerator run on propane, so we should be able to turn them on now. I know it seems overwhelming, but these things won't be so mysterious when we get used to them. They are really worth while for extended stays."

While she walks room to room, I enjoy her excitement in discovering the nooks and peculiarities of this modest island home. Soon enough we come to the bedroom, the last of the three rooms. It's small, with a double bed against the outside wall, a closet, and one dresser. I look at Ann and offer to use the sleeping bag in the livingroom. She protests, suggesting everyone slept on double size beds before queens and kings came along. The point was a good one, so I relent, trying to mask my delight. Silently, I resolve to get at least a queen-sized bed into this little room, even if I have to move one of the walls.

Our dinner, cooked on the antique cast iron skillet, completes the most memorable evening to date. Whiffs of smoke curling from cracks in the potbelly's stove pipe cloud the ceiling, enhancing the rustic setting before I belatedly open wider, the pipe flue. We walk the ridge above the quiet cove in the frosty night, marveling at the moon's perfect image reflected below us. At ten thirty, I reload the stove, adjust its draft, and make ready for bed. Ann times her entrance after I am settled, deliberately I believe, and not without maximum effect. I'd place her somewhere between Aphrodite and a contemporary model. With energy spent, and before drifting off, I resolve to forget getting a larger bed. What a dumb idea.

*

Carlos Montero eases the "Bob Cat" into reverse, and turns the wheel sharply. Inching forward, he raises the hopper and drops the final load of dirt into the dump truck. Gray clouds scud over treetops as a light drizzle threatens intensity. Two lab men work feverishly to finish gathering every bone fragment and other unnatural item from the hole before the predicted deluge confuses the terrain.

Carlos had unearthed the first bone two days before while breaking up the concrete apron. Scraping uncovered soil, he noticed what appeared to be an animal bone laying in plain sight. On closer inspection, the bone looked to be a human arm, a humerus, according to his boss. The discovery was brought to the attention of the police within the hour and began what was to become one of the biggest investigations in the town's history.

*

Wind-ruffled hemlocks slapping the side of the building wake me at seven. Still sleeping, Ann rests peacefully while I sneak into the tiny bathroom and prepare for the day. Rest-stop-green paint from ceiling to floor will be my first priority to cover next summer. The task for the morning is to check the diesel supply tank and run the generator. A glance at the fuel filters shows the owner had working knowledge of engine maintenance. Primary and secondary filters were ink-marked at the last change, fifty-five hours. Absence of rust and the general cleanliness proved the unit to be quite new.

After breakfast, we clean and do small maintenance chores during the next four mornings. Afternoons are spent walking the island end to end, digesting every bit of uniqueness. I sense Ann is completely taken with the place. Evenings feeding the stove chunks of firewood and listening to music CDs on her portable player are mesmerizing. Completely contented, we fall into bed nearly exhausted each night.

Early in the morning of the fifth day, I awake to intermittent groans from the chimney, announcing the arrival of the season's first nor'easter. By the time we get up, the storm is lashing the mainland coast with continuous white water as far as we can see. We agree that our stay on the island may be extended several days longer than anticipated.

"Is anything troubling you?" Ann inquires.

"Not really. I guess I'm just a bit tired from all the activity the last few days."

"We'll probably have to stay inside today. It's too wet and windy for me to walk the ridge," she offers.

"This type of storm will last a while," I reply. "Good time to do inside stuff, like un-sticking the back windows where the paint has glued them in place."

I can't help feeling apprehensive, like if something's going to end the contentment we've enjoyed since arriving on the island. Maybe it's the sudden arrival of the storm that's unsettling. Releasing the windows with a putty knife and hammer doesn't ease my tension, but nearly kills what's left of the morning. Washing for lunch, I hear Ann answer her cell phone from the living room. I believe the call is in error and assume it ended as she doesn't respond in conversation after her initial hello.

"Wrong number?" I ask, walking into the room.

"I know you do. Of course you can, Jenny. Try not to worry and thanks for letting us know,"

"What's that all about?" I inquire, sensing her anxiety.

Her face is ashen. Her small frame sinks into the sofa, and suddenly I suspect this has something to do with her brother.

"The town road crew discovered human remains while preparing the new sidewalk on Country Way. There's speculation the immature bones could possibly be Richard's."

She looks at me through flooding tears. Her hopeless expression draws me beside her, and I take her hand. For the first time I feel resistance, as if she wishes to be alone, not accepting my comfort.

"I'm so sorry you have to experience this all over again. I didn't tell you where it happened to spare you that constant reminder when you use that road. I knew there was a chance the remains could be uncovered, but there was as much chance they wouldn't be found. I gambled, and I guess I lost."

I begin to stand, but she holds my arm. I must be forgiven, for she again soaks my shirt with tears. She seems crushed. I wonder if we'll ever be able to crawl out from under this darkness.

"The police asked Jenny if they could take a swab sample from inside her cheek for DNA matching. I told her to do it," she sobbed. "I hope I did the right thing."

"You did fine. When we get off the island, I'll straighten out this whole affair with the authorities. Try not to worry about what we can't control. I think we'll be here for another couple of days before the seas settle down enough for Johansson to pick us up."

Ann finds a functioning weather cube inside one of the kitchen drawers. From this we get a better idea of the storm's ferocity and duration. They are reporting sixty knot gusts. It's no wonder everything on the coast is shut down. Four days of continual rain moderate on the fifth morning, so we take advantage of the break and venture outside. Scrub hemlocks and a large boulder beside the bend partially shield us from the bitter wind as we leave the porch. Strong gusts blast us head on when we reach the ridge road beside the cove. A long field of confused timothy grass swirls every which way on the hillside. Thunderous waves crash below the east wall, driving spray high above the cliff where it rides the wind across the island like salty fog. Seas break endlessly, one after the other, tumbling across the cove's entrance and effectively sealing off ferry service.

"I love watching the magnificent turbulence around us," Ann hollers across the howling wind. "It's hard to imagine how serene the island was only a few days ago."

"It'll be that way again after this storm runs its course," I reply. "It's starting to rain again. Let's get back to the porch before we drown."

Before long, the cutting wind drives us inside the cottage, in time to hear the last ring of my cell phone perched on the kitchen counter. The 207 Maine area code leads me to match it with Johansson's business card, so I punch the call-back key.

"Hello?"

"Hello, this is Holt Tilden on Cliff Island returning the call to my phone."

"Yes, Mister Tilden. This is Eleanor Johansson. Have you seen Edward?"

"No, is he supposed to be here?"

"Well, he left the harbor during the brief let-up this morning —said he was going to see if it would be safe getting into the cove. I'm worried because he hasn't called me."

"I'll go down to the cove and check right now, ma'am. Try not to worry; give me about an hour. OK?"

"I'll be waiting. Thank you, Mister Tilden."

"Edward's wife says he may have tried to get out here this morning. I can't believe he would attempt coming through that surf."

"I'm going with you."

Sheets of rain pelt us as we struggle against the ferocious wind blasting the ridge road. Most of the coastline fronting the cove entrance can be seen from this elevated plateau.

Ann tugs at my shirt sleeve and yells in my ear, "Can you see anything?"

"Not a damn thing from here, too much white water. We need to get down by the breakwater for a closer look."

While descending the slope, I can't help but notice what looks like intermittent reddish brown flashes mixed with the white foam, a hundred yards this side of the breakwater. If something had been anchored there before, I don't recall it. Getting closer, I realize this looks like the painted bottom of an overturned boat. Might this be Edward's skiff?

"Hello, hello, Edward, helloooo," I yell at the top of my voice. "Johansson, helloooo."

"Do you think that's his boat?" asks Ann.

"It's a flat-bottom skiff with a copper painted bottom, same as his. Try walking back along the beach a couple of hundred yards, and see if you can find something. I'll work my way toward the channel."

From the ridge I'd seen a large volume of flotsam collecting in the back eddy behind the line of boulders forming the breakwater. As I approach the foamy cauldron, I find various multi-colored lobster buoys washed in from the storm. Among the buoys bobbing in the relative calm are chunks of wood and plastic. My eyes quickly lock onto what first appears to be a harbor seal lying on a floating log. On closer inspection this appears to be a human, wearing a brown jacket, probably the man we are looking for. I excitedly wave my arms to signal Ann, encouraging her to hurry.

"Is it Mister Johansson?" She gasps.

"It's him all right. He seems to have a pulse, and I think he is breathing," I reply while hurriedly tugging the big log through the froth toward the beach.

"Go back and get the wheelbarrow from the shed. That's the only way we can get him to the house."

Ann sprints across the beach and I yell to her, "Don't call his wife yet."

An appendage on the log apparently snags the bottom in knee-deep water. I grab Edward by the shoulders and drag him ashore and up the sloped beach. I lay him on his back, head down, with his feet in the grass. By now I'm unsure if he is still alive. Howling wind and airborne debris prevent a meaningful examination, so I clear bits of seaweed from his mouth and begin CPR. Within minutes, traces of fluid emerge during intermittent choking and coughing. He regains consciousness and vomits when I roll him on his side.

"Look out!" Ann warns as the uncontrolled wheelbarrow tumbles down the last ten feet of rocky ledge, coming to rest beside us. The blanket and pillows she had thoughtfully brought lay scattered about in the sand.

Ed's complexion is ghostly gray and he's shaking violently.

Until now, he hasn't spoken a word.

"You ready for a ride to the house, Edward?" I ask.

He nods slightly, without taking his eyes off the rolling breakers. Ann and I prepare the pillows and help him to the front of the wheelbarrow without disturbing the blanket wrapped around him. His rattling teeth unnerve me, and I feel him vibrating inside the blanket as we guide him onto the pillows.

"I'm sure glad you thought to bring these pillows."

Turning to the loaded wheelbarrow, "You'll be in the warm house in a few minutes, Edward. Let me know if you're going to be sick again, and I'll stop."

We arrive at the cottage as the next squall dumps another deluge. Edward is unable to walk inside without each of us holding an arm. From the looks of his condition, I decide to call the Coast Guard immediately, hoping for an airlift to the hospital. The local office assures me someone will get back to me within minutes. Unsure if we should give Ed a stimulant, I decide to feed him tepid water with a little honey to warm his insides. Ann attends to this concoction as I place one of the kitchen chairs in the shower and begin the flow of lukewarm water. Still in his wet clothes, we coax him into the stall, where I support him in the chair and we both soak up the heat. Ann relieves me in the shower so I can make the call to his wife.

"Hello?"

"Hello, this is Holt Tilden again. Your husband is here with us in the cottage and is doing fine. Right now, he is taking a hot shower. He had somewhat of an accident out on the..."

"What do you mean accident?" she cuts in.

"His skiff overturned while negotiating the bar. He is now warming up in the shower, and I've called the Coast Guard to bring him ashore. They'll be getting back to me with the details in a few minutes.

"My lord! What next?" cried Eleanor.

"Don't worry yourself, Ms. Johansson. He's all right now. I'll keep you informed when we know where they will be taking him.

I hear the shower continuing to run and think the heater tank should be passing him chilled water by now. Good timing, as the shower is turned off and Edward expresses gratitude through the closed door. I relieve Ann and strip Ed bare before drying him with a large beach towel, taking care not to rub his skin excessively. (I read something about this in treating victims of hypothermia.) With a fresh set of my clothes and a bundle of blankets, he is ready to fly.

I pick up the phone on the second ring. "This is the U.S. Coast Guard, Southwest Harbor Maine, calling Holton Tilden."

"This is Tilden."

"I am calling to inform you a helicopter has been dispatched from Cape Cod en-route to Cliff Island, Maine, for the purpose of airlifting one probable hypothermia victim to the Eastern Maine Medical Center, in Bangor. There is a medical team aboard. The estimated time of arrival at Cliff Island is 4:45 EST. The rescue team expects to use a cable and basket, so have the patient suitably clothed for travel. The team will communicate by speaker from the airship. Are there any questions at this time?"

"Yes. Must we load the basket, or will a man come down with it?

"If the patient is ambulatory, you may load the basket—be sure to use belts according to the posted instructions. If needed, we will lower a medic to assist."

I'm anxious to accomplish Edward's transfer to people trained in treating near- drowning and exposure. While contemplating how we will conduct our hand-off, we hear the thunderous beat of the chopper hovering over the ridge road barely a hundred yards from our cottage. Ann rushes outside to confirm our location, while I guide Edward into the wheelbarrow and push him to the lee behind the boulder at the corner of the road. The basket is lowered to the ground, and I wheel Ed the last hundred feet. The rotor turbulence is nearly overpowering as I struggle to guide Edward through the gate and into the straps. I worry the small amount of cable slack whipping menacingly above my head may tighten at any moment, jerking the basket up before he is secure. Thankfully the pilot's steady control makes the hand-off relatively smooth, and the patient is on his way, for probably his first helicopter ride. Notice of the evacuation and the Bangor destination is relayed to Ed's wife by Ann, who assures her that his trip to the hospital is only precautionary.

Ten

Scituate Police Station, in cooperation with state and county officials, has hummed with activity since the discovery of bones under the aging sidewalk. The laboratory crew from Plymouth spent four days photographing and charting every facet of information from the unusual grave. The hole was tented and under guard until every bone and accompanying item was removed and cataloged. Records of the construction dates, compared with the Baxter boy's disappearance, has everyone convinced a positive identification will emerge. Samples of bone for DNA tests were hand carried to the Boston lab, accompanied by oral swabs taken from Jenny Osborne, considered a possible niece of the deceased.

Walt Samuelson shuffled his large frame up the granite steps of the newly completed police station. Eighteen years of retirement have slowed Walt's gait, but not his mind's agility. A full head of confused gray hair frames his heavy facial features. He's been following the news accounts in the local paper and thought he just might contribute some historical perspective to the deliberations.

"Hello, Walt, you old scoundrel," said Hennessy, the desk sergeant.

"Hello yourself, Tommy. The chief in his office?"

"Go right in, Walt. Knock, but don't spook him. He's probably got his feet up and might even be resting his eyes."

A light knock on the chief's door didn't get a response, so Walt crossed the varnished floor and eased himself into the generous captain's chair fronting the long mahogany desk. Here he resolved to wait him out, might even get a little rest himself.

Walt's eyes closed. Before he could drop off, Chief Jerome spoke. "To what do we owe the pleasure of your company, old-timer?"

Jerome had been the town's chief of police for fourteen years. Locally known as Eagle Eye for his acute observation and memory, he was respected by most of the citizens, or at least the law abiding ones.

"You got me just in time, Chief. I'd be out for an hour if you'd tried me a minute later."

"Well, you got something on your mind. We don't see you around here much nowadays. Bet it's got to do with the bone pile under the sidewalk, don't it"

"How'd you guess it, Chief? You gotta have crystal balls under that big desk of yours."

"Well, what you got Walt?"

"You weren't around here in the forties when the Baxter kid went missing. I'd been on the force about three years. Knew most of the boys around town, especially the problem ones. Baxter and Ben Griffin were two of the biggest troublemakers. If memory serves me right, they were up on some kind of burglary charges around the time Baxter disappeared. I believe the two of them ratted on each other, culminating in some nasty threats between them. There were strong suspicions back then that young Griffin had something to do with Baxter's disappearance. Try as the county did, they couldn't find anything incriminating enough to bring charges. Somebody's got to have records regarding the boys in that case, which by the way, I think was eventually sealed by the court."

"That's mighty interesting, Walt. I'll pass it along to the county fellas. It shouldn't be hard to unseal those records under the circumstances. Now I got something for you. You gotta keep what I'm about to tell you in strict confidence. You won't find this in the news, but the investigators believe they've found the weapon used in the killing. Can you imagine someone tossing a gun into the same hole as the body? Not too smart, I'd say. We retrieved a .38 special revolver under the bones, and guess what? Rust had obliterated the serial number, but inside the right hand ivory grip someone had carved a name. Here's the shocker: the name inside the grip, is Ben Griffin's dad, BG Sr. They checked it out. You may remember the old man spent thirty-five years as a police officer in Quincy. Those guys purchased their own weapons, and according to their records, Griffin had reported his revolver missing over a month before Baxter disappeared. Now we know where it went. Tell ya, that Ben Griffin already has both hands in the ringer over the assessor scandal. That will seem small potatoes when we hang this one on him."

"Think you're on to something, Chief. It'll be interesting to know what they find out from the court records on those kid's activities."

The day after Johansson was airlifted from the island, the nor'easter blew itself out, leaving huge slick-backed rollers tumbling across the bar. George Bailey called on my cell with the latest report on Jackson's progress. He also offered to bring us ashore when the seas moderated. Accepting his generosity, I told him we'd be ready on an hour's notice. We reluctantly close the cottage two days later, loading George's skiff for our departure from this peaceful and sometimes wild island, only to approach uncertain turmoil in Scituate.

Eleven

If only we had left the car radio off during our return. One of Boston's news stations interrupts our easy listening, announcing "DNA tests confirm the identity of fifty-year- old bones found under a sidewalk." The publicity confirms what we both know and pushes the door open wider for public scrutiny. Ann wants to be dropped at Jenny's, and I'm returning to the motel efficiency. As I arrive in the motel driveway, I'm vaguely aware of the Florida tag on a red Ford pickup parked in the space adjacent to my room. Once parked, I realize this is my son Michael's truck. I sit for a moment, wondering if he knows I've arrived. There's no sign of him, so I walk to the reception room door and open it. The owner's well-fed tiger cat scrambles across a stack of papers piled on the oak desk and shoots through the pet door in the outside wall. The commotion wakes slumbering Bob, whose shoes remain on the desk when his feet return to the floor.

"You're back, Mister Tilden! Did you notice we have another Tilden staying with us?"

"I see you have. How long has the boy been here anyway?"

"Came in day before yesterday, looking for you. I told him you were away, and I didn't know when you'd be back. Said he would wait."

"Which room is he in?"

"Right next to you, number 113."

"Thanks, Bob. I'll see if I can raise him."

When I approach Mike's door, it swings wide open and he invites me inside for a beer. He knows I don't drink beer. I see his room is neat as a pin. He's always been respectful of property.

"Where have you been, Dad? I've been here for three days worrying about you during the storm. Nobody around here knew where you went."

"You could have called me on the cell phone, instead of worrying, son. If I'd known you were driving all this way, I would have waited. That's if I couldn't have talked you out of it. How'd you get time off from work?"

"Don't worry about work. I've got plenty of vacation time so I took a week."

"Have you eaten dinner?"

"I had a late lunch, but I could eat something."

"Let me get cleaned up and I'll rap on your door in fifteen minutes. I know a place where we can get a light meal."

On the way to the restaurant, I fill Mike in on our trip to Cliff Island. We enter the Bucket just after 6:30, with little competition for a quiet corner table. The evening waitress takes our orders. As she leaves for the kitchen, Mike begins unloading some of his concerns.

"Do you know a body was found recently in town? According to the papers, it must have been buried sometime in the forties. Has that anything to do with the subject of your letter?"

"Yes, I know about the discovery and yes, it has a lot to do with me. You'll remember I wrote about meeting the boy's sister and my consequent decision to delay confessing to the police for the time being. Well, things have progressed to the point where, until the discovery of the bones, we had both agreed to leave well enough alone. Now, if the identity is established, it will be necessary to re-evaluate our decision."

"You haven't seen a newspaper since you got back?"

"No, What's their slant on the story?"

"They are reporting the police have a suspect, some guy named Griffin."

"Griffin! Ben Griffin?" What on earth would lead them to believe that?"

"I have no idea. I haven't followed the story because knowing they have a suspect, I didn't think it was the same case."

"Well, I'll have to straighten that out. How in hell did they connect Griffin with this?"

"Why do anything, Dad? Why stick your neck out now? Just leave it alone."

"I don't know if I can do that. I guess I'll have to wait and see what develops. You realize we could have covered all of this by phone instead of your driving all the way up here. This isn't going to be settled in the next couple of days, you know."

"Laura's been stewing about this ever since your first letter, Dad. You know how she is. I used to think she'd get over worrying about every little thing when our kids got older, but she hasn't changed. She's the one who's been pushing me to come here the most, but Sis drove the final nail. In the end we figured it was about time somebody came to see what's going on. Seems like stuff's happening and we've got no perspective on what you're doing. I know who this lady is, but we can't imagine how you've been drawn to her so quickly. It really mystifies everyone."

"So you're the emissary, sent to gather the facts."

"Yeah, I guess I am."

Our dinners arrive in time for me to gain some composure for the continuing inquisition. I'm beginning to feel maybe its best Mike came to express the family's concerns personally. He'll also be able to get a better understanding of the whole situation. I feel a tinge of remorse for keeping the kids uninformed so long and for failing to confide my deepening involvement with Ann. Two couples enter the front door and amble toward the adjacent table while kindling my annoyance.

"Look, there's one by the window," says the sharp-eyed girl ignoring the innocuous chatter of her companions.

"Bet you never had broiled scrod like this before," I comment to Mike while the young group veers toward the furthest table.

"Looks good to me—what is scrod anyway?"

"It's a small cod or haddock taken from the top of the pile for its last caught freshness. That's the story anyway."

"Getting back to the bones, Dad, what are you going to do now?"

"I'll attempt to find out how they've come to suspect Griffin. I can't believe they have anything substantial. I know the guy. He's certainly no friend, but I can't stand by and watch an innocent man wrongly convicted."

"Dad, I've tried to imagine how difficult it must be to live with this nightmare all by yourself. I don't see how you did it, especially when you were so young."

"Son, I had no choice. It was an unfortunate circumstance, not of my choosing, but I decided early on not to allow those few seconds to dominate my life.

Because of our intense conversation, I suspect other people may be listening. Observing the nearby diners, they appear otherwise occupied. Hopefully, our conversation is not being overheard. Mike expresses a thoughtful summary of the facts as he believes them to be. As I study my son, I'm consciously aware of his maturity, something I'd completely failed to recognize before.

"How much longer are you able to be away from your job?" I ask.

"I've got three or four more days before I need to start back."

"Well, that gives me enough time to show you around town. Too bad we don't have a few days to visit the cottage I'm buying in Maine."

"You're buying a cottage in Maine?"

"Yup, my uncle's old house on Cliff Island. I told you kids about spending summers there when I was a boy. Well, it came on the market, and I signed a contract to buy it. I think it will make a nice family retreat. You and your sister may use it whenever you want. That's where Ann and I were weathered in for the last ten days."

"That's great. Wish I could see it before going back. How far is it?"

"It's more than two hundred miles each way. There are no winter residents anymore, just summer folks. Maybe next year you can all come up for your vacation.

"When will I be able to meet your lady friend?"

"Tomorrow. I'll take you over there for breakfast. How's that?"

Later that evening, I call Ann, telling her we will be having a third for breakfast. She expresses enthusiasm about Mike coming and then unloads the same news about Griffin being a suspect. She agrees that we should wait and see what develops before getting involved.

*

The following morning, Ben Griffin sits in his empty dining room chair scanning the newspaper for new articles concerning him. The other three chairs, drawn back from the table, are stacked with outdated newspapers and months of unopened mail. Since his practice of massaging real estate assessments has become such a big deal in the local newspapers, he's lost contact with most of his friends and imagines enemies around every corner. Now to top it off, he's suddenly the suspect in the killing of his once best friend nearly fifty years ago. What evidence have they found, he wonders? When Dickey vanished they tried connecting him to his disappearance and came up empty. His recent unpopularity is sure to get worse since being named a "person of interest." A call to his attorney John Congdon adds this potential charge to his defense agenda, but does little to allay his fears. Resting his forehead on the table, Ben again contemplates leaving town. How could I transfer money without leaving a trail, he wonders? Where would I go? What about Social Security and identification? Envisioning the maze of details required to disappear is too complicated for him to consider today. Maybe later.

*

Michael and I pull into Ann's driveway looking forward to breakfast. She evidentially heard us coming and we find her standing in the open doorway.

"Good morning," Ann calls with a musical ring. "Michael, I would know you anywhere. You look just like your father."

"Good morning Mrs. Carlson. Thank you for having us over for breakfast."

"You're quite welcome. Come inside. Everything is nearly ready to put on, so you might as well have a seat."

The table, as usual, is neatly set with linen tablecloth, napkins, and small bowls of assorted fruit. Coffee is poured and bacon is being kept warm in the oven, while she scrambles eggs. Nothing in this house is ever out of place. Everything's in order. I wonder how we'll ever restore this serenity in our personal lives. I can sometimes feel our control slipping away.

"How long are you able to stay in town, Mike?" Ann asks.

"I'll leave the day after tomorrow. Took a week's vacation plus the weekends, so I've only four days left and it's a two-day trip."

"Why don't we plan to have dinner here tomorrow evening then? Does that fit into your plans, Holt?"

"Yes, that's fine if you want, but wouldn't you rather go out instead of working in the kitchen?"

"Not really. I think it will give us more time to share with Michael about what's going on, don't you?"

"Yeah, that's fine. The two of us are going for a tour of

the town today. I'll be able to fill Mike in on the cast of characters. Probably stop for lunch at the Bucket where he can meet Jenny. Would you like to join us there?"

"Not today, thanks. I've got to stay at the shop until we finish sorting the van load that came in yesterday."

"Do you work every day?" asked Mike.

"No, just volunteering three mornings a week."

I sense Mike's reluctance to address the reason he drove all the way to New England. I am tempted to broach the subject, but decide instead to keep the conversation light; hoping the two of them will part amiably.

After breakfast, I drive Mike to the harbor. The view toward town from Lighthouse Point is impressive. A chilly wind creates tufts of white chop on the dark blue water. Mike has seen pictures of the harbor, but was unprepared for its beauty. I brought him here for the privacy and salt air, where we could sit on the rocks and talk candidly without interruption.

"So, what do you think about Ann?" I asked.

"She's very nice, Dad. How serious are you two?"

"Very serious, son. I hope to have a long future with her if we don't get derailed by this ugly situation."

"I hope you aren't, Dad. She seems to be a charming lady. Are you going to stay put for a while to see how things develop with this Griffin guy?"

"I think so. You know he's a detestable individual as far as I'm concerned, but if the authorities bring him to trial, I'll have to intervene."

"You'll confess what happened?

"I don't know how I can avoid it."

"There's gotta be a better way than that, Dad."

"How can I let an innocent man be convicted for something he didn't do, Mike?"

"Well, for one thing, he probably won't be convicted on such flimsy evidence."

"Maybe he won't, but the trial would ruin his reputation,

even if he is acquitted."

"Sounds to me like he hasn't much of a reputation to ruin. Why not let this run its course, considering he is such a rascal. You can always come in at the last minute if he's convicted, can't you?"

"Yeah, I suppose I could. I'll have to think on that one."

"You planning on marrying her?"

"I wondered when you would come up with that one. We were very close to deciding that before this erupted. I sure can't predict anything right now. Would our marrying bother you?"

"No, I don't think it would. I can't speak for Sally, but I'm fine with it."

"Thanks for the support, son. If we do decide to make it permanent, I'll need your help with Sally. She can be damn obstinate sometimes."

"Tell me about it, Dad."

*

Within three days, the District Attorney succeeded in having the Baxter and Griffin files unsealed by the court. Those records revealed that two of the town police officers had caught the boys exiting a neighborhood home through one of the back windows at 6:30 in the evening of October 3, 1947. The transcripts indicate that the two juveniles were questioned separately regarding this and other recent break-ins. Further examination revealed Griffin's answers were in sharp conflict with that of his friend. Separate notations were found in the file of two police officers, who overheard Griffin threatening his friend's life while the boys argued in front of the police station. The threat, "If he caved into the cops during questioning," was noted in quotation marks. In the back of the folder was a yellowed letter addressed to Chief Winston Homer from Mrs. Elmore Baxter, requesting police assistance in "ending the constant harassment of her son Richard, by Ben Griffin."

Chief Jerome received portions of both transcripts and notes from the county. Back in his office, he placed the material into a second file marked "Baxter/Griffin." Somewhat disappointed with the meager quantity of information, he at least had given something substantial on the case to the county office. It would be their determination if enough evidence exists to prosecute Griffin successfully in court.

*

Standing erect after sitting on the rocks a couple of hours becomes a painful maneuver. I feel the time well spent. We candidly covered more subjects than I expected. I accept Mike's compromise and nearly promise not to offer a confession unless Griffin's erroneous guilt looks assured.

The half-mile walk to the Bucket brings us by the marina and fish docks jammed with activity. We stop to examine one of the last eastern-rigged draggers in existence. A solitary fisherman sits on a keg, mending a big net hanging from the gantry. This aft pilothouse vessel requires the net to be deployed over one side. The rig was popular until stern trawlers edged them out in the late forties. I can see by his lack of inquiry, Mike's fascination with commercial fishing is minimal. We continue our trek to the restaurant without further investigation. Before we enter the dining room, I caution Mike that Jenny doesn't know of my involvement in Baxter's demise.

Introductions are made at the Bucket, and Jenny tells me Griffins' been seen cruising in his truck on Front Street for more than an hour. I try to minimize any threatening significance, suggesting this is probably an outlet over concern regarding his legal problems.

"How long are you here for, Mike?" asks Jenny.

"I'm leaving the day after tomorrow."

"Well, I hope this thing's over quickly for mom's sake. I don't want our names bandied about town like mom said happened when her brother disappeared."

I notice the limited exchange between Jenny and Mike, like the impending turbulence was a black hole neither of them wanted to look into. I'm also worried myself about the colossal mess we're all going to be faced with in the coming months. Observing little exchange between the two, I suggest Mike and I leave to attend to some last minute details prior to his departure.

Twelve

It's been a month since Mike departed for home. Deciduous trees have shed the last vestiges of color. Storm windows replace screens, and wood smoke curls from chimneys. Dusk creeps through town by four o'clock. A half hour later it's dark. Dickey's grave is capped, and the new sidewalk is complete. Thanksgiving's on people's minds; only three more weeks.

I've been renting an apartment in the adjoining town since Mike left. The expenses are less and I've more privacy away from the motel.

My relationship with Ann remains steady and passionate. We see each other every day, eat meals, and take walks. Scant progress on Dickey's discovery is leaked to the press. We are all in the dark.

Ben Griffin remains on the loose, but he's rarely seen in town. We guess the case against him is too weak to prosecute. Jenny is worrying over her mother's health. I know she feels I too am unsettled. She's still unaware of my prior involvement with her deceased uncle. If it's necessary to eventually expose myself, I'll wish I'd leveled with her earlier.

Due to the lack of news on the case, I am astonished one morning when opening the paper in Ann's driveway. Stunned, I feel helpless, imagining our whole future exploding. Oatmeal is bubbling on the stove when I enter the kitchen.

"Good morning, lover," she chirps.

With her kiss on my neck, I drop into the chair and lay the folded paper on the uncluttered table. I must prepare her before she sees it.

"Morning, sweetie. The driveway was frosty on the way in. I'm glad you made hot cereal this morning—it's going to be a chilly day."

"What's new in the paper?"

So much for preparation.

"Looks like they picked up Griffin," I reply.

Ann slips into the chair beside me, and together we read the headline, "Griffin suspect in boy's death." Below the caption is a massive front page display of the article. "Benjamin Griffin of Scituate was arrested yesterday by Plymouth County deputies on suspicion of the murder of Richard D. Baxter in 1947. Griffin, a former town official, is also currently charged with property assessment irregularities." Page two continues the story, yielding little new information other than one shocker: "Items found at the gravesite include a revolver owned by Griffin's father."

"A revolver?" I exclaim. "I don't believe it. What revolver? How could they find a gun? There wasn't any gun, and he wasn't shot!"

"I don't understand. How would they find a gun?" Ann inquires.

"I don't know. I really don't know. If there was a gun recovered, it had to have been placed there later. Maybe the gun part is untrue. You know how newspapers scramble the facts half the time. Doesn't Jenny's husband know some guy at the Plymouth courthouse? Maybe he knows something about this?"

"Bill's boyhood friend works there—he might be able to help. Bill and Jenny are coming for dinner tonight. We can see if he can find out anything. He's going to wonder, though, why we're so interested. Are you considering going to the police now?"

"No. Don't worry. I'll wait and see what happens before getting involved. We must both agree before I commit to anything."

Ann smiles and holds my arm. Breakfast is eaten in acquiescent silence while we try to imagine what's coming next.

"Are you ready for our walk?" she asks. "Or do you want to forget it?"

"I'm ready. The fresh air will clear our heads."

We notice the fleet is in when we descend the hill to Front Street. Fishermen are preparing their gear. Bait is forked into waiting barrels in boats tied to the float. Diesels idle, belching smoke rings from dry exhausts. Ann slips on a flounder frame. I grab her arm before she hits the pavement.

"Let's stop at the Bucket before we go back," she suggests.

Jenny waves to us when we seat ourselves at one of the small end tables.

"Have you seen the paper?" she asks, unfolding the front page while approaching.

"Yes, we read it at breakfast."

"I'm worried everyone will be looking at us Mom, and asking questions again."

"Don't pay any attention to them, dear. We'll just have to endure this until it's over."

"Ben Griffin gives me the creeps. I hope he doesn't come in here again if he gets out on bail."

"Don't concern yourself with any of this, Jenny. Mr. Griffin probably won't be walking around here for some time, if at all."

It may be my imagination but I feel most of the breakfast patrons are discussing the news revelations and sneaking glances in our direction.

"It's natural for people to be curious about something like this, honey. A few people may even know who you are and glance your way. Just ignore them. You have nothing to be ashamed of. Now we'll see the two of you for dinner tonight, OK? Hadn't we better be heading back, Holt?"

"Ready if you are."

Outside the restaurant I realize my tense feeling while in Jenny's presence must be because we're concealing my involvement in the death. I dislike keeping the truth from her, but I believe the decision Ann and I made to keep it between the two of us was the best option.

"What do you think about the gun discovery?" Ann inquires.

"Well, I've been trying to think of another possible reason it found its way into the grave. The most likely one is that Dickey had it on him all the time. If he had a hand gun in a pocket or his waistband, it would have been out of my sight. The news story didn't state if the gun was loaded or not. It also didn't say if it was the suspected murder weapon. I wonder why."

*

A day earlier, at 4:30 in the afternoon, two unmarked cars were parked on opposite sides of Blossom Street in front of Ben Griffin's property. Sheriff John Chambers and one of the three deputies accompanying him occupied the vehicle closest to the suspect's house. An occasional auto whisked by, elevating a thin fog from the drizzle-saturated road. Deep throated exhausts rumbled from a black pickup slowing for the turn one block east. Both unmarked sheriff's cars appeared empty when the truck made the last turn into the driveway. The driver's door opened. When Ben's feet contacted the ground, he came face to face with a three-man arrest team. Minutes later he was on his way to Long Pond County Jail.

*

Eight days before the arrest, County Court Judge Oscar Bean had signed a search warrant for Griffin's residence. One of the items gathered by detectives was a rosewood cigar box containing sixteen knives of varying descriptions, each with some form of defect. One knife of special interest was a slender switchblade, missing a small piece of green colored bone handle. Among photographs taken by the detectives, were pictures of antique and contemporary knives arranged on the den wall.

*

Late into the night Ben repeatedly paced the twelve foot depth of his holding cell. News of the police discovering his dad's gun in Dickey's grave was shocking, but having the police rummage through his home was the last straw. Expecting his lawyer to arrange bail in the morning, Ben reclined on the jail cot and began mentally constructing his next move. He was again reminded of the axiom "fight or flight." This meant he must dig in and fight the charges, or leave town and be on the run forever. He knew his defense would require admitting he was on the scene when Dickey was attacked. He could claim he was following Holt Tilden, knowing the two were going to fight, and he wanted to watch. He could testify that when his best friend fell to the ground, he ran off, terrified he might be considered a suspect. The other option is to finalize his plans and leave. This is the ultimate Plan B end game he's had in his head from the beginning. For weeks he's been hurriedly making preparations for an exit. What a rotten surprise having the police finding his dad's revolver with the body. I wonder what else Dickey stole from us, he thought. There's a real possibility the police could win a conviction, coupling his dad's gun with the body and producing old police records revealing their mutual hostility. For now he will continue preparing alternate paths to side step his responsibility. In the morning he'll see what his attorney advises.

"John Condon, Esquire." Ben sat in the courtroom beside his lawyer, staring at the bold letters on the brass nameplate affixed to the briefcase by his feet. This was the arraignment Condon had been priming him for this morning. The bailiff called the case by docket number at 10:45. Judge Bean greeted

Robert Myers, the D.A., and defense attorney Condon, then followed by inquiring if the defense would agree to wave the reading.

"Agreed."

"Mister Griffin, how do you plead?"

"The defendant pleads not guilty."

"Would you like to address bail for the accused, Mr. Myers?"

"Your Honor, in capital cases, I normally request bail be disallowed. For the record, the defendant is already on bail for an alleged offense coming to trial in eighty-four days. I acknowledge the defendant's lifelong ties to the community, but considering the nature of this charge and the lack of any living family in the area, I respectfully request bail be denied."

"Mister Condon?"

"Your Honor, I am fully cognizant of the charge against my client. He is, however, a businessman of long standing in our town. He has served more than twenty years in the assessor's office and provided countless jobs to area residents in his surveying company during the last thirty years. Prior to the previous month, Mr. Griffin had never been arrested nor had a traffic infraction lodged against him. Unfortunately, he is currently under this county's indictment for certain alleged irregularities in the assessor's office. This charge we consider politically motivated and we plan a vigorous defense. Considering my client's lifelong ties to the community and lack of any prior record, I believe he is not a flight risk and respectfully request he be released on minimum bail."

"Bail in the amount of one-hundred-thousand dollars is hereby granted. Bailiff, please escort the defendant back to his cell until surety arrangements are made."

The double doors swung wide open at 11:35 the following morning, expelling Griffin and John Condon into the brisk November air.

"I'm making an appointment with Lambert and Sons in

Boston to handle your defense, Ben. We'll be lucky if they will fit us into their schedule. They're the best in the business, and you're going to need them."

"You want me to go with you?"

"Negative. Go home and make as little noise as possible. The less you're seen the better. You know, I should charge you extra for getting your bail without a monitor. If I didn't know the judge and prosecutor well, you'd be wearing a bracelet and confined to your home."

"If you're going to charge me for it, make sure you itemize the bill."

"Don't you worry. It will be hidden in conferencing."

As the two men separate on the street corner, Ben is determined to implement Plan B in the coming week.

Thirteen

The likelihood of being found guilty for Dickey's demise prodded Ben to seriously finalize preparations for the quick departure he'd been hoping to somehow avoid. Researching the subject "how to disappear without being found" on the computer had given him all the basics. He had enough sense to do this investigation using one of the Internet cafés in Providence, Rhode Island, thus avoiding an electronic trail to his home. According to the published experts, it should take at least four months to do proper planning and preparation. He had to accomplish this in much less time. He'd begun by purchasing two expensive forged identities from an agent in Boston, including what the gentleman claimed were foolproof social security numbers. The first identity's post office address was established in the nearby town of Brockton. The second identity address was a post office box in Dallas, Texas.

Maximizing hand-carry cash without raising suspicions in town proved to be time consuming. Stocks and bonds were gradually liquidated. Several gold bullion coin purchases were made from separate companies. Each buy was kept under twenty-five-thousand dollars to avoid a transaction record with the federal government if it was indeed required. Of this he wasn't sure, but he wasn't taking any chances. His home mortgage had been satisfied ten years earlier. Attempting to sell the property quickly would certainly raise a flag. An out-of-town mortgage broker solved this dilemma by quietly arranging a refinance, netting him eighty percent of the current appraised value. Good enough, he thought. By the time he was bailed out of jail, Ben had accumulated $981,786 in U.S. and Canadian cash and gold bullion coin. Because of his advanced age, he reasoned he could stretch this all the way to the end.

Griffin's arrest and subsequent release on bond the week before weighs heavily on my conscience. I'm tempted to turn myself in but wonder if it's too soon. I constantly worry about the negative impact on our families. Ann's stoicism appears genuine. She's expressed complete faith in whatever decision I make. I've solicited her advice only to receive concurrence with my desires in return. I'm certain of her sincerity but sometimes wish she would offer alternatives for debate. Perhaps I'm too anxious to intelligently plan our next move, but it's no excuse. I'll begin informing the family after telling Ann tonight.

"What smells so good?" I inquire, entering the kitchen.

"It's your favorite—fish chowder. Bill and one of his friends brought over two fresh haddock they caught this morning."

"Great! Do you have any salt pork in the freezer?"

"It's on the counter, thawed and ready for the knife. Wouldn't be right without salt pork," she adds.

As I dice the fat into small bits in silence, I try to imagine speaking the words I know will dampen the evening. The ventilated metal cover rattles over the pot's rim, while boiling water transforms the contents into dinner. Bits of pork fat sizzle in the frying pan. Ann slides the mixed corn bread batter into the hot oven.

"I'm thinking it's time to turn myself in."

"I know this has been on your mind, Holt. You've been awfully introspective the last few weeks. If you really think it's time, you know I'll support your decision all the way."

"I can't put it off any longer, Annie. It's all I think about.

I know he's a rat, but I'm as bad as he is if I let the system punish him for something I did.

"Have you thought about when you want to do it?"

"Not exactly. I've got to tell the kids first. I believe they're half expecting I'll do this anyway from the letters I receive. I don't know how we'll break it to Jenny and Bill though. Now I wish we'd told them earlier."

"I think we should inform them together, with me opening the conversation," Ann suggests.

Age is definitely catching up with me. My emotions lie just below the surface. Ann's compassion through our whole association often overwhelms me. It overtakes me now as tears flood my eyes, and I mutely turn away, embarrassed. She moves to my side and puts her arms around me. Her concern isn't enough. I quickly move, rub my eyes and damn my weakness.

"Let's take a walk," I suggest looking toward the ceiling.

We remove our meals from the burners and step out the back door into the December evening's darkness. My emotions are calmed by elapsed time and cold air. For a while I regain my composure.

"There's got to be an end to it sometime. I am so tired of carrying this guilt all my life. I should have done it long ago. It was an accidental death. The most it could be judged is manslaughter. I should have turned myself in when it happened. I'll never shed the guilt. I'm sick of it. Sick, sick, sick. The tears return. I feel like a child. How about putting dinner on the table? I'll be inside in a minute."

With an "I love you," she nods and returns to the house as I wipe my eyes with both sleeves and briskly walk around the building to dry my face. Inside of ten minutes I'm somewhat collected and re-enter the house.

Laura answers the telephone when I call at 9:30 the following morning. It's Sunday, and Mike picks up the second phone. I inform them of our decision to go to the police and explain the reason it must be done now. I receive little resistance.

"You know what is best, Dad. Do you want us to come up?" Mike asks.

"That's not necessary, son. You have your own affairs to tend to without spending time here. These things are apt to be drawn out anyway. I'll call you daily if needed, to keep you informed.

"We aren't going to tell the kids about it until things are more settled," Laura injects.

"I think that's a good idea. I'm calling Sally and Jim now and suggest they do the same with Chloe. She's much too young to assimilate this.

I'm surprised at the lack of resistance by the kids. They must have had second thoughts after the initial shock of my involvement settled in.

"When do you want to have Jenny and Bill over?" I ask Ann.

"How about tonight after dinner?"

"Let's do it," I reply. By the way, I'll have to inform Tom and Arlene before going to the station. I've been holding Tom off long enough. He's been ribbing me about becoming a permanent resident, but he's never inquired again about the business that brought me here. He must be puzzled."

"Would you like me to accompany you tomorrow?

"I was counting on it. You and Arlene are like sisters."

It's not unusual for us to stop at the Phillips' house if we see their car parked in the yard. We arrive just after 11:00 a.m., catching Tom as he hauls the last bag of oak leaves to the compost pile.

"I was about to go inside for coffee. Arlene made a fresh pot. How about joining us?"

"Sure, Tom, we'd like to. We do have some news to share with both of you."

"Great! You're getting married!"

Ann smiles, and receives a friendly hug from Tom. She

then moves perceptibly closer to my side.

"No, Tom, we aren't getting married, not yet anyway. Is Arlene inside?"

"Arlene, honey, Ann and Holt are here. We're coming in the kitchen."

She enters through the dining room. "Hi gang. What's going on?"

"Morning, Arlene. I'm sorry this isn't the blissful visit to announce our engagement. We've come instead to confide to you tragic circumstances in which we're involved. I know you'll keep what we are about to say in strict confidence for now. You may remember during the gracious evening gathering when I first arrived, that I vaguely mentioned coming here to settle some old business? Well, it's about to be settled.

"First of all, I'll never be able to repay you both for your friendship and kindness in introducing us to each other that night. We were attracted to each other the very first moment. This was the beginning of a rejuvenated life for both of us. I was certain you hadn't observed the shock I incurred in your living room when discovering Ann was the little sister of the boy I accidentally killed so many years before."

They are both speechless. The room is completely still.

"Her brother Dickey had been bullying me for several school years. His last attempt occurred in the woods behind his recently discovered grave. He came at me from behind, I struck him once with a metal rod, and he fell. I ran home, not knowing if he was just hurt or something worse. I didn't tell anyone, nobody. I buried him after midnight two days later. No one ever knew, nor did they ever suspect me in any way. I'd only told my wife, Marion, eight years after we married. Ann has been aware of this unfortunate incident for some time. She has her own dark memories of abuse by her brother. The reason I returned to town was to admit my guilt and hopefully find peace. We decided to table my confession after falling in love and considering our similar paths. Ben Griffin's arrest for a crime he didn't commit has altered our plans. He's a son-of-a-bitch, but in this case, an innocent one. Go ahead guys, it's your turn."

"God, how old were you, Holt?"

"Thirteen."

The two women are holding each other and sobbing. Tom and I gravitate to opposite ends of the room, each looking for a distraction.

*

Ben studied the topographical map spread on the seat beside him. This revealed every hill and hollow, including the abandoned granite quarries west of Quincy. The old quarries, now filled with water, are favorite dumping grounds for stolen vehicles and an occasional body, compliments of Boston's underworld. The particular pond Ben was searching for should lie directly ahead. As he approached the area he'd circled on his map, he decided to park his truck on level ground near some sumac bushes and scout the area on foot. He found the pond straight ahead, over the edge of a twenty-foot wall of loose granite. His approach would necessarily be from the right side to avoid a small stand of beech trees populating the ridge. Ben tied his crumpled white handkerchief to a maple sapling to mark the best approach to the pond's edge. Back in his truck, Ben sat staring at the quarry's edge. Certain the authorities could successfully convict him, he had no other choice but to leave. The finality of his decision to abandon the only home he'd ever known was overwhelming. He knew his biggest blunder was in keeping that damn knife. What a stupid mistake that was. The image of Dickey's bloodied body lying among the wet branches has haunted him ever since. Even though he rarely thought about it, behind a thin veil, the nightmare was always with him. Ben leaned over the steering wheel and closed his eyes. The veil lifted, and Dickey lay dazed before him. Ben's switchblade was open and plunging repeatedly into the boy's chest. He could still recall his fist bouncing from the resilience of the boy's ribs. His reason for the attack was almost forgotten, but he assumed Holt

Tilden would be blamed. Who would have thought that creep probably buried the body?

Three days after visiting the quarry, Ben appeared in town at 7:30 in the morning. A night's dusting of early-season dry snow swirled behind his pickup as he slowed to a crawl on Front Street. Santas and sugar canes dangled from catenaries across the road. Patrons nodded shy recognition as he browsed in the newspaper store just to be seen. The filling station attendant would attest to his presence, after witnessing Ben's clean-up of intentionally spilled fuel. Cigarettes from the drug store, turnovers from Cobbler's Bakery. He was in town to be noticed. This would be the last day Ben would traverse his beloved birthplace.

*

"Hello. This is Chief Jerome."

"Chief, this is Holton Tilden, here in town. I need to meet with you on a matter of extreme importance regarding Ben Griffin's prosecution."

"How about coming in at ten tomorrow morning, Mister Tilden?"

"I'll be there, Chief. Thanks."

I press Ann's name on my cell phone to inform her of tomorrow's date with the chief. She insists on accompanying me to the station. Jenny and Bill will be over after dinner. Ann says they have a big surprise. I think Jenny is pregnant. Tom has requested I stop by and give him a hand in the morning to move his cradled boat to the side yard for the winter.

After breakfast I drive across town and find Tom has two rows of planks already laid across the lawn. He emerges from the building carrying a couple of pinch bars.

"Thanks for coming over, Holt. There's a barrel of short rollers in the garage and a hand truck inside the door. I drag the loaded device across the yard and purposely spill the contents onto the lawn. We jack up the forward cross-bearer and Tom shoves one of the maple rollers under the starboard corner. The process is repeated until each skid is supported by four rollers.

"I made an appointment with Chief Jerome for tomorrow morning," I offer.

"So you're going through with it."

"Yup, ten o'clock."

"I wish there were a better way, Holt."

"Me, too. Wouldn't be so bad if I was saving someone's ass besides Griffin's."

"Yeah, that has to make you think twice."

"Grab the other bar so we can work both sides together."

Another hour's work placed the boat beside the garage for the winter. Before leaving, I promise to call Tom after meeting with the chief.

Dinner is nearly ready when I arrive at Ann's. She's been watching for my car and has completed preparations except for grilling the fish, which is my job. I detect her contained excitement as I enter the room.

"What do you think the surprise is?" I ask.

"I don't know. What do you think?"

"I told you, they are pregnant."

"Oh, I don't think that's it. I would have known if she was."

"So, how would you know?"

"I just would—a mother knows those things. I'd really be surprised if I'm wrong on this."

"OK, we'll just have to wait until they deliver their news."

The split mackerels take only minutes to grill. After we're finished eating, we linger at the table, venturing guesses as to what the surprise will be. My money stays on pregnant. The kids arrive soon after the dishes are done.

"So what's the exciting news?" Ann asks.

Bill begins, "I met my friend Homer for lunch today—he's the guy working in the courthouse. During our conversation he happened to mention some unreleased details about evidence collected in the Griffin case. The most unusual item was a broken piece of knife grip found in the hole matched a damaged knife discovered in Griffin's collection. The investigators also think his dad's unearthed revolver was not involved in the death. The gun's cylinder was fully loaded and additional live ammunition discovered in a tight cluster, indicating they may have been in a bag or pocket during burial. The prosecution believes the gun and shells were in the possession of the deceased. Bill doesn't mention anything about a head wound, and I don't dare inquire.

Casually observing Ann's face as Bill finishes, I sense her growing comprehension matching my own.

"Thanks, Bill. That's welcome information, and I appreciate you bringing it to us."

Bill unknowingly divulged news that will change our lives forever. I'm in shock and need time to assimilate this. Everything I believed before about Dickey's death may be untrue. He must have been alive when I left him. I did nothing wrong. I think burying the body may be a technicality at this point. Ann quietly crosses to the far side of the room, handkerchief in hand. The kids politely excuse themselves and leave. I approach Ann from behind and encircle her in my arms.

"How about getting some wine and I'll light the fire."

Logs crackle and pop behind the wire screen, while we lie sprawled against pillows on the braided rug, staring into the multi-colored flames.

"Can you believe this?" she asks.

"I don't know. It sure sounds promising. I wonder if Ben's going to involve me in his defense. If he does, he'll be admitting his presence at the scene."

"What about your appointment with Chief Jerome tomorrow?"

"I'll cancel it. On second thought, I'll postpone it for a while and see how things evolve. I can always go in later if it's necessary."

We chat into the night about all kinds of possibilities before us. Ann's eyes begin to cross and then close. Chilled by the decayed fire, we awaken at 2:30. We finish the night in her bed.

Fourteen

*

Heavy rain pelted Griffin's bedroom windows the morning of his planned departure. By 4:30, lacking any sleep, he was dressed and loading the two suitcases containing personal belongings and his clothes onto the front seat of the truck. The chosen route, he'd driven days before on a trial run. Traffic at five in the morning was comparatively light. In just over an hour he reached the city. Both suitcases fit snugly into a Greyhound locker at Boston's terminal. His leather bag of assets would travel with him, along with his money belt. Overhead, the blackened sky was graying as dawn advanced.

The drive to the quarry took twenty-five minutes. By then, there was enough light to negotiate the rutted dirt road to the field he had previously chosen. The truck rolled to a stop. Ben stepped into the rain soaked grass and proceeded to the white marker he'd tied to a branch. He moved to the edge of the pond. The water level appeared higher than before, about eight feet below the edge. With his bag of valuables on the ground, he moved the pickup to within ten feet of the quarry's edge. From the back of his truck, he retrieved a twenty-two inch piece of 1x4 wood and wedged it between the brake pedal and the driver's seat. A flat shale stone, selected for the purpose, was propped against the accelerator and adjusted to increase the engine's rpm to 1500. Ben glanced around the field to assure he was alone and then scanned the cab for personnel items. Seeing none, he stood to the side and yanked on the string holding the brake block. His beloved truck flew off the cliff and splashed head first into the pond. In seconds, the half-submerged truck was bobbing fifteen feet from the wall. As he watched bubbles rise from all sides, he realized he should have rolled down the windows. The driver's door had slammed closed during the crash. As Ben stood watching his truck gradually sink, the finality of his plans overwhelmed him. Twenty minutes later, he was hitchhiking on Rt. 3 to Boston, the leather bag tightly held under one arm.

*

Ann slumbers in dreamland all night while I fitfully lie awake adjusting to our new reality. My mind randomly wanders through distorted events of childhood and the present. Annoying images keep repeating themselves. Walking around the house in the middle of the night doesn't help. Three hours of sleep begin sometime after 4:00 a.m. Awake by seven, I'm drawn to the aroma of fresh coffee. Breakfast is on the table by the time I'm dressed and enter the kitchen.

"Morning, sweetie. Sleep well?" Ann inquires.

"Not so much. I noticed you sawing wood the entire night."

"I was dead tired. I didn't even realize you were restless."

"That's because I was quietly pacing the kitchen floor half the time."

"Are you worried, or are you excited?"

"Both. I've been thinking the best way, may be to cancel my appointment with the chief as early as I can this morning. I'm trying to come up with a reasonable excuse."

"I've thought about that, also. Why not tell him you had some ideas regarding the case, but since making the appointment, they've proved to be false?"

"Sounds like a good idea. It's true and its simple. I'll do it."

"So what else is worrying you?"

"Well, assuming last night's information is correct, I've been trying to imagine how Griffin's prosecution might proceed. He'll either plead innocent, denying he was ever present at the scene, or he'll try to somehow shift the blame on me. You can see that I'm not completely in the clear yet."

"Don't worry yourself. Whatever happens, we'll get through it together."

Her confidence lightens my spirits, and we ready ourselves for the morning walk.

While descending the hill toward the harbor, I imagine the two of us exploring Cliff Island next summer. I'm really anxious to begin restoration of the cottage and yard. Ann appears to be as interested as I am about spending more time there. I wish I could be sure she's genuinely excited, and not simply trying to please me.

"Are you thinking about the cottage?" she asks.

She's a mind reader. "Yes, I am. How'd you know I was daydreaming about it again?"

"When you are quietly staring into space and nodding your head a little, I know you're planning something."

"Well, I was wondering what to do first and how much time we could spend there."

"How about all summer? We could close the house and move up as soon as the season begins."

"Are you serious? All summer?"

"Yes, I am. I would even consider staying through the winter if you want."

"You're a sweetie. I hoped you would fall in love with the island, but let's not get carried away. Winters there are no picnic. You'll notice all the residents are now summer only. The storm we witnessed was only a sample. Can you imagine the same wind with the temperature well below freezing?"

"I'm only dreaming out loud. How many months would we be able to stay?"

"I'd say spring can be pretty nasty with endless rainy days. That would be dreary, I think. We could go in early May, but June 1 would be better. Fall is nicer, with September having some of the best weather if you don't mind a chill in the air. I would guess things might wind up by the end of October. That gives us five months, might even stretch it to six."

"I'd love to do it. Why don't we plan on it next year?"

"I've already begun. Here's a list I've been carrying in my wallet, things I want to change and add to the building. I hope you like to paint."

*

Ben's familiarity with New York City is damn near zero. What he does know was gleaned from newspapers and television. He's a stay-at-home Yankee. Been to Florida once, flew down for two weeks and hated it. Filthy pavement and trampled gum greet him as the bus moves to the departure bay for new passengers. Rounding the corner, he's suddenly accosted by a dark mustached guy, motioning him to a taxi cab line while barking angry unintelligible bursts. Ben's perplexed nodding encourages the cab purveyor to advance the next vehicle, and he opens the door. Reclined in the cab's back seat, Ben salutes the gentleman who responds with a shaking fist.

"Where ya headed?"

"The airport."

"Which one?"

"The big one.

"They are all big."

"How about the closest one?"

"You got a ticket?"

"Not yet. I'll buy it when you get me there."

"Kennedy it is."

Thirty-five minutes later and forty-five dollars poorer, Ben maneuvers his travel bags to the Northwest counter. His destination: Seattle, Washington.

"Here's your bag checks and ticket. Your flight leaves

gate seventeen at 4:20 p.m. The total is $958, Mr. Alford. Mr. Alford? Sir, that will be $958. Would you like to put this on your card?"

"No, ma'am, I'm paying cash today."

Can't wait to use my final identity, Ben thought as he walked to the reception area. These name changes can be tricky.

Ben considered the two-year-old red Jeep wagon purchased in Seattle as marking the beginning of his final adventure. If he ever needs to move quickly, the wagon's capacity would hold whatever personal belongings he may collect in the next few years. The small notebook went back into his breast pocket after choosing the Jeep's color. The little book contained every trick he could think of to avoid capture. His vehicles of choice had always been Fords, and they were always black pickup trucks. This red Jeep was certainly out of character. He had also never been known to buy a used vehicle. All according to plan, he thought.

After spending a week camped in a cheap tourist motel on the edge of Enumclaw, Washington, he decided the town nicely fit his notions of a safe hideaway. The elderly Ms.Worley had nearly exhausted her rental listings before bringing him to the remote cabin ten miles from the town's center. Her enthusiasm about this particular property waned as her van left the pavement and climbed the hill over loose gravel to the five-acre parcel. A small weathered building lay just ahead.

"As I mentioned on the phone, Mr. Edwards, this is really only a hunting camp. I'm uncertain if it would be sufficient for year-around living. The present owner converted it from a camp to a summer retreat five years ago," she explained.

Adam Edwards, Adam Edwards, that's me, Ben thought. I've got to think like an Adam Edwards and forget Benjamin Griffin. Attempting to conceal his interest, he casually inquired about the cost of electricity and the condition of the well pump and water quality. He examined the camp-like interior while noting the strong wood smoke aroma from the cast iron stove while Ms. Worley loudly recited property attributes from her printed flier. The rectangular building's exterior was natural western cedar, and battened seam construction. The front wall bore two double hung windows symmetrically located on each side of a windowless planked door. The weathered cabin blended nicely with a background of Tall Oregon Grape and Snowbrush. Common Chokecherry, another bush he was unfamiliar with grew next to a small out-building on the east side. He was drawn to lease the place as soon as he spotted it from the driveway. His final decision was to be delayed until he could walk the acreage by himself later that afternoon.

*

"Holt, Holt, could you come in for a minute?" Ann called.

"What is it?" I ask, entering through the kitchen doorway.

"Bill called minutes ago. His friend Homer, at the courthouse, called him this morning saying Ben Griffin was officially reported missing yesterday. He expects this to be revealed in the newspaper tomorrow morning."

"Why am I not surprised? I don't believe the court imposed any meaningful restrictions on his release. Ben's not the type to hang around gambling for an acquittal."

"What do we do now?"

"There's nothing to do. This doesn't affect us at all. They may or may not find him, but either way, it shouldn't be a problem for us. On second thought, if they never catch him, he'll always be assumed guilty and the whole nightmare will be over, perhaps without the messy disruption of a trial."

The following morning, both newspapers covered the latest revelation. They offered, however, no new elaboration, only repeating what was revealed in the caption: "Griffin last seen in town ten days ago."

Fifteen

Most of the folks following Griffin's case were up in arms that he had been granted bail. Some questioned why he'd been released without restrictions or monitoring. A few vented their frustrations in letters to the editors. County officials and the bonding company investigator were carefully examining personal associates of Griffin and whatever information could be constructed from his financial records, in an attempt to pick up the trail. Weeks led to months, as investigative laboring produced stacks of what appeared to be useless paper.

Thirty miles north of Scituate, a special task force of the Boston Police Department was concluding a year-long criminal investigation, culminating with raids on various enterprises in Boston's North End. Three luncheon eateries were believed to be fronting gambling and money laundering operations. While sorting through records removed from the Hanover Street location, investigators uncovered tangible evidence that one enterprise was also producing false identifications. On the second of May, five months after Griffin disappeared, the Scituate police chief answered his phone.

"Chief Jerome? Lieutenant Murray with the Boston PD. I'm calling to inquire about your progress in locating one Benjamin Griffin as posted missing last December."

"I'll tell you lieutenant, we're no further ahead than when we began. Why do you ask?"

"Our boys have uncovered information from a fraudulent identification mill that may be helpful in your efforts to locate the suspect."

"That may be the first lead we've had since he skipped. What have you got?"

"Bits and pieces right now, Chief. We are mainly interested in other facets of their operation and how they are tied to similar North End shops. We found a couple of telephone numbers in with their phony IDs. I believe one of the numbers belonged to the man you're looking for. There may be enough information here to determine his assumed identity. We've got everything concerning this part of the operation in two boxes. You're welcome to have someone pick through it."

"What's the best time to see it?"

"Anytime. Ask for Sergeant O'Neil or me when your man comes in. I've already informed the state police, considering their investigative responsibility in homicide cases."

"I'll be there personally tomorrow morning, Lieutenant. Thanks for the information.

*

Ben Griffin slid two number eight shells into his Lefever 20-gauge double, as he walked toward the tree line behind his rented cabin. Since arriving in Washington, he'd cultivated a taste for wild doves. Due to the non-native bird's fertile breeding lifestyle, the Eurasian Collared dove season in the state remains open year round and is without bag limits. The birds, considered invasive since migrating from the Bahamas to Florida and moving west in the nineties, are so abundant in town, that hunting is encouraged by most owners of otherwise posted property. If a few protected Mourning Doves fall during a hunt, no one complains.

Today's quest begins at the east side of Ben's cabin and follows the gradual slope down to a swath of red mountain heather proliferating in a shallow ravine. Without aid of a bird dog, Ben must flush the birds by his own intrusion. This morning, scattered incoming birds crisscross overhead from all directions. As he turns toward the road for his next shot, Ben observes two men coming through the field straight toward him. He cautiously lowers his shotgun, contemplating the visitor's intentions. They don't appear to be dressed as locals and exhibit the look of authority, most likely law enforcement. Two additional men dressed in police uniforms suddenly emerge from the tree line to his left. Ben's breaths become increasingly frequent and deep. He becomes nauseous. His jaw aches under his chin and excruciating chest pain drops him to his knees by the time the intruders reach his side.

*

George Bailey idles his lobster boat against the float, holding it with a gaff while we toss our dunnage forward.

"Figured we'd see you people sooner or later this year. I heard you bought your uncle's cottage."

"Yes, I did, and thanks for the lift. We're going to be staying at the place on and off all summer. Can you tell me who to contact about tying a dinghy here for the season?"

"Yeah, Jack Bagley, old Clyde's nephew is the harbormaster. He collects the dock fees and mooring charges from transients. You'll see him running around in the gray work boat with Harbor Master painted on both sides."

"Watch your hand, Annie! Don't get it squashed against the float," I caution.

"How was your winter, George?"

"Not bad at all this year. That nor'easta, when you guys were here last fall, was the worst blast we had all winta."

George starts the engine and drops into reverse, pulling the boat off the face of the float, and backing it into the onshore wind. With the helm reversed we rotate one-eighty and head for the island.

"You know anyone available for part-time work at the cottage?" I ask.

"How much work you got?"

"I'm doing most of it, but I could use someone occasionally to help with the heavy lifting."

"I'm available. Call me on the cell with a little notice, and I'll work it in during my regular trips." We enter the cove's glassy calm sheltered from the wind and land our craft against an otherwise empty float. Summer has barely arrived on the island. Greenery is only beginning to awaken from winter dormancy.

"Need help carrying this stuff to the cottage, Mista Tilden?"

"No thanks. Just leave it in the pile for now. We'll be making a couple of trips with the wheelbarrow after we open the house."

I'm somewhat surprised by the desolate appearance of the little building as we round the bend in the road. Left on its own through the winter, the house literally shouts "abandoned."

We drop our first load on the porch, and immediately Ann places a call to Jenny to announce our arrival as she'd requested.

"Hello, sweetie. We're at the cottage. Everything's fine here. Yes. Who told you? Please tell me from the beginning."

"Ben Griffin is dead, Mom. He was found in Washington State. He died of a heart attack during his arrest. It was in the paper this morning. Didn't you pick one up before you left town?"

"No, no. We left before dawn."

"I tried to reach you earlier, but your phone must have been off," she continued.

"Yes, I just turned it on. I'm sorry. Anything else? I bet this is the talk of the town today."

"It is. It's on the TV and radio news. Evidently the police somehow discovered his alias and consequently found him living in a remote town in the mountains.

"Thanks for the information, Jenny. I can't wait to tell Holt. He went down to the float to get another load of supplies just before you called."

"Bye, Mom. I'll let you know if I hear anything else. Bill and I will be up in two weeks to see the place."

With Jenny's pronouncement that Ben Griffin is dead resounding inside her head, Ann runs toward the cove, only to meet me halfway back. Out of breath and panting, she shares the news.

"It was in the papers this morning. When they approached him, he apparently died of a heart attack. He was living somewhere in the mountains of Washington. This is good news, isn't it? I mean good for us, not Ben of course."

"It means we don't have to be looking over our shoulders anymore," I reply. "Yes, it's good news. Of all the possibilities I'd considered and worried about, I never expected it would be resolved this way." I suddenly feel relief, finally unshackled from a lifetime of remorse.

"We're going to have a glorious summer, and when it's over, this cottage will be a showplace, Holt. Just wait and see."

"How about having a house-warming party right here, along with a wedding?" I offer.

Her immediate concurrence comes with an extended hug and more tears cascading down my neck. I'm buoyed by anticipation of unlimited possibilities, while masking a little uncertainty. We've already shared our secret with Tom and Arlene. I hope the expectation of live lobsters once in a while, will keep them quiet.

About The Author

Glenn F. Higgins began life in 1934, forty miles from where Richard Higgins, his grandfather ten times removed, settled at Plymouth Plantation in1630. Primarily educated in New England schools, with a little of Florida thrown in, he married his high school sweetheart at age twenty. Both son and daughter swam as infants, sharing family hours on and in the waters of Cape Cod Bay and the islands. A designer and builder at heart, he, with several associates, founded an antenna company in 1963 which occupied much of his time until retirement in 1998. Several years of live-aboard cruising from New England to Florida and the Bahamas moved the couple to regain shore ties on Pine Island.

The writing bug struck after settling into their present home in the seclusion of Bokeelia's palm groves, and began with family and foreign travel memoirs. Membership in Pine Island Writers Inc. on the island, encouraged continued efforts, leading to the creation of the book you are holding, the first short novel to cross the finish line.